'Where a Man Is And Lets Her Know By Kissing Her,' John Said.

Before Merideth could stop him, he closed his mouth over hers.

The capture was so complete, so unexpected, she felt her knees weaken, her heart slam against her ribs.

'And sometimes even touching her,' he murmured against her mouth as he pulled her body against his.

Willing herself not to respond, she took in a shuddering breath. 'If you think I'm going to spend the next several months playing nanny while being pawed by you, you've got another thing coming.'

He drew his head back just far enough to meet her eyes. '*You* might call it pawing,' he said, his eyes burning into hers, 'but down here in Texas, we call it something else…'

Dear Reader

Summer is here, and Desire™ is bringing you a line-up that simply sizzles! Diana Palmer fans will be happy to find that she's back this month with **Man of the Month** Simon Hart. This stubborn hero has only one weakness, beautiful Tira Beck, and she has secretly been saving all her love for him!

We have more of your favourite mini-series this month, too. In the second of **The Cutler Family** series, Kent Cutler is once bitten, twice shy—but Brianne Gainsborough is determined to win him round. And in **The Rulebreakers**, Amelia Russell is ready to break some rules of her own after a passionate night with bad boy Ben Palmer.

If you love baby stories, you'll enjoy reading the new tale from Anne Marie Winston, where Frannie Brooks is hired as a 'baby consultant' by a man who inherits an orphaned child. And another baby leads to the last wedding in **The McCloud Brides** series from Peggy Moreland. Finally, don't miss the rags-to-riches story *Overnight Heiress*.

Happy reading!

The Editors

A Sparkle in the Cowboy's Eyes

PEGGY MORELAND

*First published in Great Britain 1999
Silhouette Books, Eton House, 18-24 Paradise Road,
Richmond, Surrey TW9 1SR*

© Peggy Bozeman Morse 1998

ISBN 0 373 76168 6

22-9907

*Printed and bound in Spain
by Litografia Rosés S.A., Barcelona*

PEGGY MORELAND

is a natural story-teller with a sense of humour that will tickle your fancy, and Peggy's goal is to write a story that readers will remember long after the last page is turned. Peggy frequently appears on bestseller lists. A native Texan, she and her family live in Round Rock, Texas, U.S.A.

Other novels by Peggy Moreland

Silhouette Desire®

A Little Bit Country
Run for the Roses
Miss Prim
The Rescuer
Seven Year Itch
The Baby Doctor
Miss Lizzy's Legacy
A Wilful Marriage
*Marry Me, Cowboy
*A Little Texas Two-Step
*Lone Star Kind of Man
†The Rancher's Spitting Image
†The Restless Virgin

Silhouette Special Edition®

Rugrats and Rawhide

*Wives Wanted!
†The McCloud Brides

To my good friend Willie Ferguson.
A survivor whose positive mental attitude inspires us all.

One

Merideth lay back against the warm stones, letting the sun seep into her skin to work its healing magic on her body, on her mind. A month had passed since she'd arrived at the Double-Cross Heart Ranch, battered and bruised, both physically and emotionally.

The bruises on her body had faded now, but those on her heart were still tender, a constant reminder of her loss. A son, she had been told, born much too early to survive.

Tears budded in her eyes and blurred the clouds drifting across the blue sky above her. She'd brought him home with her and buried him in the family plot next to her mother. Now they lay side by side—the mother she'd never known, and the child she would never hold. Placing him there had seemed fitting somehow, and it eased the ache a little, for she knew that her mother was in heaven to greet her grandson, to gather him close within her angel wings and to watch over him.

Merideth closed her eyes behind the dark sunglasses, squeezing back the tears. Even though she was home, back on the Double-Cross and surrounded by family, she felt so alone. So utterly and terribly alone. There was no child to lavish her love on, no husband with whom to share her grief. There was only Merideth. Merideth McCloud. Soap-opera star extraordinaire. The woman whose face and body men all over the world lust after…the same face and body that women all over the world despised her for. Her life-style was envied, her wealth whispered about over cocktails….

She almost laughed out loud.

She had no wealth. The life-style she'd chosen had robbed her of that. Clothes, jewelry, travel. The good life. That's what she'd sought when she first moved to New York City. Fame, adoring fans, her name bandied about in gossip columns, linked with those of wealthy and handsome men. She'd wanted excitement, too, and adventure. And she'd had it all…but in retrospect it all seemed foolish, meaningless when stacked up against what she'd lost.

But regrets were senseless in Merideth's opinion, and only a crutch used by the weak and foolish to atone for their mistakes. Merideth was neither weak nor foolish. She was a McCloud. She had the McCloud spirit, the McCloud pride. She was a fighter, a survivor. She'd suffered other tragedies in her life and triumphed. She'd survive this one, too.

But how? she wondered. She kept her money problems secret from her sisters. She knew that both Sam and Mandy would willingly give her the shirts off their backs if she asked, but she wouldn't. Her pride wouldn't let her, not when her sisters had succeeded where she had failed. They'd spent their inheritances both wisely and frugally, with an eye to their futures, while Merideth had squandered hers selfishly and foolishly.

They'd chosen the men in their lives with the same wisdom, the same care as they'd chosen their investments, men with integrity, men who loved and lived with a passion as wide as the Texas sky. Mandy had Jesse. Sam, Nash. But who did Merideth have?

No one…at least not now.

She'd chosen the men in her life in much the same way she'd spent her inheritance—foolishly, basing her selections on image, on power, not on the person within. Her last and biggest mistake had been Marcus. Her producer, her lover, the father of her child. A man with wealth and connections, a powerful and handsome man. A man without a conscience or scruples, a man without a heart or soul.

Angry with herself for even thinking of him, she shoved the thought away and focused again on her most pressing problem.

Money. Or the lack thereof.

She needed a job. But where? What? She didn't want to go back to New York. She couldn't. But she had no other skills to offer. What else could an actress do but act?

A sigh shuddered through her and she rolled to her stomach, blocking out the depressing thoughts. How could she contemplate the future when she hadn't successfully dealt with the past, when at the moment, even the present seemed too much for her to deal with?

John Lee Carter reined his horse to a stop high on the cliff above the spring-fed pond, looked down…and almost fell out of his saddle. Expecting to find stray calves, instead he found a woman—a gorgeous, naked woman—stretched out, sunbathing, on one of the smooth limestone boulders that concealed the natural spring feeding the small pond. Blond hair haloed a stunning face with features so perfect they seemed unreal, as if shaped by a sculptor's clever hand.

Perspiration pearled on her skin and pooled in the valley between her breasts, drawing his gaze there. He let his eyes drift along the graceful lines of her body, taking in the swell of breasts, the smooth stomach, the deep curve of waist. She lay with one knee raised, shadowing a nest of blond curls at the juncture of her thighs. An arm draped carelessly across her forehead shaded her eyes further from the bright sunlight.

Merideth McCloud.

Even at this distance, John Lee recognized her. He'd heard she was back in town. He'd also heard the reason why she was there. He shook his head, bracing his hands against his saddle horn, his gaze lingering on the woman below. Seemed even the rich and famous couldn't escape the tragedies in life. As a man who'd served his own time in the limelight, John Lee knew that all too well.

Talk was that she'd suffered a nervous breakdown after losing a baby. But John Lee knew better than that. Oh, he didn't doubt she'd lost a baby, but he did question the part about her having a nervous breakdown. Not Merideth McCloud. She was way too strong for that.

Always ripe with the juiciest news, the local grapevine had it that Merideth had come home alone to bury her baby. Though the lack of a husband shocked some, it didn't faze John Lee. This was the nineties, after all, and more and more women were opting for single motherhood.

As he watched her, he thought he saw a shudder pass through her. Then she turned, shifting onto her stomach, blocking his view of her face. But her backside was almost as interesting as her front. Dimples winked at him from above a nicely rounded butt.

John Lee chuckled as he turned his horse for the well-worn path.

Merideth always was a flirt.

"Don't you know that it's a crime to sunbathe nude in Austin?"

Startled by the male voice, Merideth jerked up her head. Though a cowboy hat shaded the face of the man sitting on the tall bay standing opposite her, she recognized him immediately. That cocksure grin. Those broad shoulders, thick thighs. Sun-bleached, sandy-blond hair that brushed his collar. Eyes as blue as a summer Texas sky, that always seemed to tease. Features carved into a breathtakingly handsome face.

John Lee Carter.

His grin deepened. "They've even outlawed skinny-dipping at Hippie Hollow on Lake Travis. A crying shame, too, if you ask me. Personally, I've always thought of the human body as kinda like art, something meant to be appreciated."

Another time, Merideth might have agreed with him, even flirted with him and invited him to join her on the warm rock.

But not today.

Today she felt nothing but resentment that he'd invaded her privacy and disrupted her solitude, something she so rarely found on the Double-Cross.

Planting her elbows on the rock, she tipped her sunglasses to the end of her nose. From the devilish gleam in his eye, she could tell that he was enjoying the fact that he had caught her at a disadvantage—him being fully dressed, and she wearing nothing but her birthday suit. She narrowed an eye at him. "Well, it's good to know that some things never change," she offered dryly. "John Lee Carter is still seeking cheap thrills."

He tossed back his head and laughed. "And you're still as sassy as you always were."

He continued to grin at her, and Merideth knew that he was just being ornery. He'd love nothing better than to watch her squirm in embarrassment at being caught sunbathing nude, but Merideth refused to give him the pleasure. She met his gaze squarely, evenly. "Are you going to sit there all day gawking, or are you going to turn your back so that I can get dressed?"

He squinted up at the sun as if pondering the question, then dropped his gaze to hers, a slow smile crooking one corner of his mouth. "I don't know, the view's pretty good from up here. But, then again, I wouldn't want you to burn. How much sunscreen are you wearing?"

The look Merideth shot him was glacial. "Not enough." She stabbed a finger at the bridge of her sunglasses, shooting them back into place on her nose, then grabbed for the towel beneath her. Quickly, she sat up, wrapping it around her…but not before John Lee caught one last glimpse of those luscious breasts.

He let out a low whistle that turned Merideth's frown into a scowl. With a huff, she tucked one corner of the towel between her breasts to hold it in place, then tipped her face up to his. "What are you doing here, anyway? This *is* private property, you know."

"Just picking up a few strays that wandered onto Double-Cross land." He plucked a toothpick from his hat-band and stuck it between his teeth, then lazily rolled it to one corner of his mouth. "What are *you* doing here? You decide to give up acting and take up ranching?"

She quickly glanced away. "Maybe," she replied, fixing her gaze on something in the distance.

John Lee blinked hard to make sure it was Merideth he was talking to. *Maybe?* His comment had been meant as a joke, one he figured would get a rise out of Merideth. Hell, she hated the Double-Cross, always had, and had hightailed it for New York right after her old man died. He was sure her stay on the Double-Cross was a temporary one, that once she'd fully recovered from the accident he'd heard she was involved in, she'd haul ass right back to the Big Apple and her career there as an actress.

"You're giving up acting?"

"Maybe. I haven't decided yet."

Maybe, again. What in the hell is going on with her? he wondered as he stared at her profile. Though her chin was tipped in that I'm-the-queen-of-the-manor look she wore so well, he sensed more than saw the quiver in it.

She's still grieving, he realized, then wanted to kick himself for his own insensitivity. "I was sorry to hear about your baby," he offered gently.

She dropped her chin to her chest and with trembling fingers began to pluck at the towel that draped her thigh. Her murmured "Thank you" was so low it was almost lost on the soft breeze that carried it to John Lee.

She looked so pitiful sitting there that John Lee regretted even mentioning her loss. "Are you staying up at the ranch house?" he asked, hoping to shift the conversation to a less sensitive topic.

A sigh lifted her shoulders. "Yes, though it's awkward since Mandy and Jesse married."

"You've stayed there before with them," he reminded her.

"But Sam was still there then. Now she's married and living with Nash on his ranch." She drew her knees up, hugging them to her chest. "She's at the Double-Cross almost every day, but it's just not the same. I feel as if I don't belong there anymore, that I'm a burden to everyone, though they assure me I'm not."

They were spoiling her again, John Lee decided. He'd grown up with the McCloud sisters and had witnessed firsthand how both Mandy and Sam coddled their little sister. They were probably so busy hovering over Merideth, smothering her with attention, that they didn't realize that they were only making things worse for her.

Merideth didn't need spoiling. What she needed—in his mind, at least—was a swift kick in the butt to get her up and running again. As her friend, he figured it his duty to give her that kick.

"So why don't you move out?" he challenged her. "You're a big girl."

She looked up at him in surprise. "Move out? But where would I go? What would I do?"

That she would even ask him those questions convinced John Lee that he was right. Merideth needed help, and fast. A distraction, he decided. That's what she needed. Something to take her mind off her loss, her problems.

And he had just the distraction she needed.

He braced a forearm over the saddle horn and leaned down. "How about dinner tonight? My place. I'll throw a couple of steaks on the grill, ice down a few beers and we'll talk about your options. Whaddya say, Merideth?"

"I don't know, John Lee," she murmured, resting her

chin on the tops of her knees. "I'm not very good company right now."

"So when were you ever?" He chuckled when her chin came up, her blue eyes sparking fire. Yep, he could still get a rise out of her. Not all was lost…yet.

"Seven sharp," he told her. "Be ready." He wheeled his horse around and loped away before she could refuse his invitation.

Merideth sat before her mirror, studying her reflection. Her eyes were dull, her face pale—in spite of the hours she'd spent sunbathing—and her cheeks hollow, a result of the weight she'd lost.

Grief was not a pretty sight.

With the hand of an artist she applied makeup, shading some areas of her face, adding color to others, until she'd created the mask she needed—one that her sisters would never see beyond.

But could she fool John Lee?

When he'd caught her sunbathing nude earlier that afternoon, her body wasn't all she'd unintentionally bared to him. She'd bared her soul as well.

But not tonight. Not ever again. Merideth McCloud never displayed her weaknesses *or* her desires. She'd learned early in life that doing so gave people power over her…and no one would ever control her again.

With a defiant shake of her head, she pulled the band from her hair and combed her fingers through the thick blond locks, lifting and adding height and volume.

Rising she took a deep breath, mentally preparing herself for the upcoming performance, the same one she'd given every day since she'd arrived at the ranch to keep her sisters from worrying about her, from guessing the depth of her grief, the extent of her financial problems.

As she did when she took on any role, she closed her eyes and focused inwardly, emptying her mind of every thought, her heart of every emotion, until she was hollow, a vessel waiting to be filled, a mound of clay waiting to be shaped.

Merideth McCloud. The most difficult role she'd ever taken on. The youngest of Lucas McCloud's three daughters. The one without a care in the world but her own wants and desires. The one with the attitude.

Slowly she felt the tension ease from her shoulders and the energy begin to surge through her. She opened her eyes, one eyebrow arching a little higher than the other, her lips already curving into the sultry pout she was known for. She winked and the reflection winked back.

She'd found her, the old Merideth, and she'd be her...at least for the moment.

"Does she know?"

Mandy shook her head, but kept dusting, nerves making her movements jerky. "I don't think so. If she did, surely she would have said something."

"Should we tell her?"

Mandy stopped her dusting and turned to Sam, who had, as each of them did when one of the three was in need, responded to Mandy's call for help. She caught her lower lip between her teeth and worried it. "If we do, I'm afraid she won't go and I really think this might be good for her. She thinks she's fooling us with this front she's putting up, but I know she's hurting inside. She needs to get out more and be around other people. Moping around here all day certainly isn't helping."

"Yeah, but is going to John Lee's the answer?"

Mandy wrapped the dust cloth around her fingers and nervously twisted. "I don't know. I just don't know."

"What don't you know?" Merideth asked as she strolled into the room. Dressed in a gauzy calf-length dress, she trailed a light, seductive scent in her wake.

Mandy shared a quick worried look with Sam. Frantically, she searched for a response, anything but the truth. "I don't know where all this dust comes from," she said with a sudden inspiration, quickly turning to push the cloth along the mantel once again.

Merideth raised her arms above her head and stretched catlike. "I don't know why you even bother," she said, stifling a bored yawn. "The furniture will just be covered again tomorrow."

"Yes," Mandy agreed, "but there'll be one less layer of dust."

Merideth shifted her gaze to Sam. "What are you doing here this late?"

"Making a vet call." The lie came easily to Sam, because it could have so easily been the truth. She was often called to tend to a sick animal on the Double-Cross. She gave Merideth the once-over, pretending she didn't already know her younger sister's plans. "What are you all gussied up for?"

With a resigned sigh, Merideth sank onto the sofa next to her. "I'm going to John Lee's for dinner. I saw him while I was out sunbathing at Cypress Pond. He caught me—well, off guard," she said with a flutter of her hand that sent the gold bangles at her wrist clinking together musically. "When he offered the invitation, I didn't have my wits enough about me to refuse before he rode off."

"You don't want to go?" Sam asked.

"Heavens, no!"

"Sure you do," Mandy insisted as she ran the dust cloth over the mantel one last time. "It'll be good for you to get out and have a little fun for a change."

Merideth angled her chin to peer at Mandy from beneath a neatly arched brow. "With a playboy like John Lee?" She snorted. "I seriously doubt an evening with him will be fun." She fanned her fingers in front of her face, checking her nail polish for any nicks. "Exhausting, maybe," she added thoughtfully, "but definitely not fun."

"Exhausting?"

"Yes, from dodging all his passes."

Mandy laughed and dropped down on the sofa, squeezing in between her two sisters. "You make John Lee sound like some sex-crazed maniac."

"He is."

"He is not!"

Merideth turned to her. "How many girls in high school claimed that they'd slept with him?"

Mandy lifted a shoulder. "A few."

"A few hundred, you mean. And how many women's names did you hear linked with his during his stint with the NFL?"

"A lot, but then *your* name's been linked with quite a few men, as well. I certainly hope that doesn't mean *you* slept with them all."

Merideth lifted her chin. "Certainly not." She adjusted the band of emerald-cut diamonds on her finger, a gift from one of those men, a millimeter to the left. She smiled smugly. "But then, I have much higher standards than John Lee Carter."

John Lee shifted uncomfortably in his Porsche's leather bucket seat, trying his best to find some more room for his cramped legs. He bit back a curse, the pain in his knee threatening his usual good mood. Six hours spent at his desk updating the ranch's ledgers, and an-

other four spent on horseback scaring up strays from the
brush had left him stiff-legged and crankier than a two-
year-old in desperate need of a nap. By the time he'd
made it back to the house to get cleaned up for his date
with Merideth, his knee was swollen and throbbing like
a bitch in heat.

Damn that three-hundred-pound ape of a defensive
guard who clipped me just below the knees, he cursed
silently. Five minutes, he told himself. Five minutes
alone with him and John Lee would make that son of a
bitch pay for prematurely ending his football career and
for the pain he'd live with for the rest of his life.

The pain was so intense, he'd considered calling Merideth to cancel his invitation for dinner and soaking in
his whirlpool instead. But then he remembered how much
she needed his help…and how much he needed hers.

He stole a look at the passenger seat where Merideth
sat, her elbow propped on the edge of the open window,
her eyes shaded by dark sunglasses while the wind played
havoc with her hair. Maybe he should have canceled, he
thought belatedly. Dealing with Merideth was always
tough and tonight he really didn't feel up to the challenge.

Too late now, though, he told himself as his ranch
house came into view. With a sigh, he pulled the Porsche
up in front of his home and climbed out, then had to wait
a second before he was sure his knee was going to support him. "Damn car," he muttered under his breath as
he slammed the door behind him. "No bigger than a
matchbox. I ought to sell the damn thing and buy me
something with some size to it."

Merideth tipped down the visor and studied her face
in the lighted vanity mirror placed there. She touched the
tips of her middle finger and thumb to the corners of her

mouth and drew them together, blotting her lipstick. "Why don't you?" she asked, turning to him.

"Because I like it," John Lee snapped disagreeably, then headed for the front door of his home.

Merideth frowned at his back. And wasn't this just her luck? It looked as if she was condemned to spending an evening with Dr. Jekyll and Mr. Hyde. The man who'd teased and laughed and taunted her that very afternoon, was gone and she was left with this scowling, grumpy-faced bear. With a sigh she sank back against the seat.

When he realized she wasn't following him, he stopped and half turned. "Well?" he asked impatiently. "Are you coming or not?"

Without sparing him a glance, she flipped the visor back into place and lifted her chin. "I'm waiting for you to open my door."

John Lee turned to face her. He propped his hands on his hips, cocking one hip higher than the other, and scowled. "You aren't gonna try that prima-donna crap with me, are you? You're a big girl now. You can open your own damn door."

She turned her head slowly, one brow arched point-edly. "I thought the code of the West dictated that cowboys must treat women like ladies. I guess I was wrong."

"Oh, for God's sake," John Lee grumbled, and rounded the car to jerk open her door. "Get out," he ordered impatiently.

"My, aren't we friendly tonight," she replied dryly. She lifted a hand, waiting for him to take it.

With a low growl, he grabbed her hand and all but yanked her from the seat. "Are you satisfied now?"

With a look of disdain, she turned her back on him. "What you lack in finesse, you certainly make up for with your macho-jock-turned-cowboy charm."

Her sarcastic remark had the same effect on John Lee as a shot of cortisone had on his knee. Forgetting all about the pain and discomfort in his leg, he tossed back his head and laughed. Macho-jock-turned-cowboy. What a description! And one only Merideth could come up with. Yep, he told himself. There was hope for her after all. He slung an arm around her neck, crushing her hairdo, and headed her toward his house. ''Darlin', you'd be surprised what kind of finesse us macho-jock-turned-cowboys possess.''

''Mmm-hmm,'' she replied doubtfully as she slipped a hand beneath his arm and freed her hair.

Once inside, John Lee tossed his hat onto the entry table. ''Mrs. Baker, I'm home!'' he yelled.

An older woman bustled from the kitchen, stripping an apron from around her thick waist. ''Thank goodness,'' she puffed, mopping the apron against her damp brow. ''I'm 'bout ready to drop.'' She wadded the apron into a ball and stuffed it into a purse she retrieved from the coat closet, pausing long enough to stare at Merideth for a moment. When Merideth lifted a brow in reply, the woman turned away with a disapproving huff.

''The salad's in the refrigerator,'' she informed John Lee, ''the potatoes in the oven and the steaks on the grill. I set the timer, but you'll need to turn 'em in about five minutes. I've fed the—''

John Lee grabbed her elbow, cutting her off, and hustled her toward the door. ''I sure appreciate you taking care of everything, Mrs. Baker. And don't you worry that pretty little head of yours about a thing. I can handle it from here. See you in the morning.''

Before Mrs. Baker could catch her breath, he'd closed the door in her face. Then he turned and pressed his back against it as if locking out the devil himself. He looked at Merideth and forced a smile. "That was my house-keeper, Mrs. Baker."

"Oh?" Merideth picked up a glass sculpture of a horse from a marble-topped table and held it to the light, study-ing the colors. "And here I was thinking she was your mistress." She smiled sweetly at him as she replaced the sculpture, then turned and wandered into the den.

Nervously jiggling change in his pocket, he trailed her. "There's something I need to tell you," he began. "You remember my sister Sissy, don't you?"

Merideth glanced back over her shoulder. "Well, of course, I remember Sissy."

"Well, about a month ago, she—" But before he could explain further, a whimpering sound came from behind the kitchen door.

Merideth turned in the direction of the sound. "What was that?"

John Lee caught her arm and dragged her along behind him. "That's Cassie," he explained as he tugged Meri-deth through the kitchen door behind him. `

"For pity's sake, John Lee," Merideth fussed, trying to wrench free. "You're going to break my—" She stopped, sucking in a shocked breath when her gaze fell on the source of the whimpering noise. There was a play-pen on the kitchen floor and inside it sat a baby, her face red, her mouth opening for a full-blown wail.

Unable to move, Merideth stared, her breath locked tight in her lungs.

"This is who I was going to tell you about," John Lee explained. He moved to the playpen, scooped up the baby and swung her high in the air. She immediately stopped her wailing and filled her hands with his hair, laughing, her chubby legs chopping at the air.

"Merideth," he said, settling the baby on his hip, "I'd

like you to meet Cassie. Cassie, my girl,'' he continued, rubbing his nose against hers, ''this here is Merideth McCloud, the sex kitten who stars in that soap Mrs. Baker likes to watch in the afternoon.''

Merideth tore her gaze from the baby to stare at John Lee. ''She's yours?''

''Yes—no. Well, you see—'' At that moment the timer went off, signaling that the steaks were ready to be turned, and the baby started howling again. John Lee thrust her toward Merideth. ''Take her while I check the steaks.''

Her eyes riveted on the baby, Merideth locked her hands behind her waist and started backing toward the door. ''N-no. I—I can't.''

John Lee danced a moment, from Merideth to the playpen then back, trying to decide what to do. Finally he plopped the baby in the playpen and started out the back door. ''Keep an eye on her,'' he ordered, aiming a finger at Merideth's nose. ''I'll be back before you can say scat.''

She stretched out a hand. ''John Lee, wait! I—'' The door slammed behind him.

The baby continued to wail, and Merideth closed her eyes and flattened her hands over her ears, trying to block out the sound—the same sound that haunted her dreams at night. In the dream, her baby, her son, cried out for her, his pitiful wails tugging at her heart. She would run, searching and searching, following the sound, but he always remained just out of sight, just out of her reach.

The crying continued, rising in intensity. As hard as she tried, Merideth couldn't block out the sound. She forced open her eyes to find that the baby had knotted her fingers in the mesh sides of the playpen and was hauling herself to a wobbly stand. Fat, frustrated tears streaked down her face and dripped off her chin. Releasing her tentative hold on the mesh, the baby held out her arms to Merideth.

Emotion pushed at Merideth's throat, choking her, while pain ripped through her chest like a knife, slashing at her heart.

She pressed her fists against her lips, fighting back the tears, until her knuckles turned as white as her face.

Oh, God, she begged silently, *please help me. I can't bear this. I can't!*

With a broken sob, she whirled and ran from the room.

John Lee stepped into the kitchen just as the front door slammed. Seconds later his Porsche's powerful engine roared to life. Over it all he heard Cassie's lusty squalls.

"Damn," he muttered as he shoved the platter of steaks onto the counter. "Damn. Damn. Triple damn, hell!"

Merideth raced down the highway, the wind whipping her hair around to sting her face. Tears burned behind her eyes and clotted her throat, but she held them back. She wouldn't cry. Not yet. With each shift of gears, she pushed the accelerator harder against the floor, trying to outrun the sound of the baby's cries, the plea in the child's watery eyes, the tiny arms stretched out to her.

But she couldn't. They echoed in her mind and squeezed at her chest until she felt as if she were suffocating beneath them. Why had John Lee done this to her? she silently cried. She'd always known he was ornery, but she'd never known him to be cruel. Surely he must know how fresh her pain was, how difficult it would be for her to see another baby so soon after the loss of her own.

At look-out point, she spun the steering wheel to the left, careening onto the small paved space, then slammed on the brakes. Jerking on the emergency brake, she sank down in the seat, the pain in her chest deep and debilitating.

Her son. Her infant son.

She'd seen him only once, the glimpse as quick as the sweep of a butterfly's wings, the memory hazy as if viewed through a winter morning's fog. She'd never held him close to her heart, never cuddled him to her breast. Yet, she had yearned to. Oh, God, how she had yearned to.

The wad of emotion that filled her throat rose higher, choking her. With no one and nothing but the cactus and the rocks and the darkening sky to witness her grief, Merideth covered her face with her hands and let the tears fall.

Two

John Lee sat on the sofa in the McClouds' living room with a sleeping Cassie cuddled against his chest. Mandy and Sam sat opposite him, the look in their eyes damning.

"I know it was the wrong thing to do," he said regretfully. "Or at least I do now. But I swear I was only trying to help Merideth. I thought if she and Cassie met up, they might be good for each other. You know, both of them having suffered a loss, and all."

He sighed in frustration when Sam and Mandy continued to glare at him. Hell. He'd said he was sorry. What was there left to say?

The roar of his Porsche on the drive outside saved him from having to make any more attempts at an apology, for it made both Sam and Mandy leap to their feet. He stood, too, and stretched out his free arm to stop them from rushing to the door. "If you girls don't mind," he said, "I'd like to talk to her first."

The two exchanged a glance, then stepped back, silently indicating their agreement.

"In private," he added. He held out the sleeping baby to Mandy. "Would you mind looking after Cassie for me while I talk to Merideth?"

Mandy stretched out her arms, her expression softening as she took Cassie from him.

Sam continued to glare at him. "If you upset her again, John Lee, I swear I'll—"

He held up his hands in surrender. "I'm not going to do anything but apologize. You have my word."

Not wanting her sisters hovering over Merideth while he made his amends, John Lee headed for the front door and the porch beyond, hoping to intercept Merideth before she reached the house.

Dusk had settled over the landscape since his arrival, leaving the porch in long shadows. He paused there among them, watching Merideth's approach, noting the droop of her shoulders, the heaviness in her step. He wished he could see her expression, too, but her hair curtained her face and dark sunglasses masked her eyes.

When she reached the foot of the porch steps, he took a deep breath and stepped from the shadows. She froze at the sight of him, then firmed her lips and started past him.

John Lee took a step sideways, blocking her way. "I'd like to talk to you, if I could," he said quietly. "To explain."

"There's nothing you have to say that I want to hear." She started to go around him again, but this time John Lee caught her arm, holding her in place. When she tried to twist free, he tightened his grip, his fingers digging into her flesh.

"Five minutes, Merideth. That's all I ask."

She yanked off her sunglasses to glare at him. "That's right, John Lee. When charm fails, use muscle. Isn't that what you cowboys usually do to get your way?"

More than her words, it was the red, puffy eyes and the tracks of tears through her makeup that made John Lee release his hold on her. "I'm sorry, Merideth. I never meant to upset you."

Fresh tears welled in her eyes and she fought them back. She wouldn't let him see her cry. "Apology accepted. Now go home to your baby and leave me the hell alone."

"She's not my baby."

Already turning for the house, Merideth stopped.

"She's my niece."

Slowly she turned to face him. "Sissy's baby?"

"Yeah."

Though the news surprised her, it didn't soften Merideth's anger with John Lee. She lifted her chin, her look one of contempt. "I always considered Sissy intelligent, but she certainly has displayed poor judgment in her choice of babysitters."

John Lee heaved a sigh. "I'm not baby-sitting. I'm Cassie's guardian. Sissy's dead."

The blood slowly drained from Merideth's face. "Dead?" she repeated in a hoarse whisper.

John Lee thinned his lips, fighting back the emotion, the memory. "Yeah. She was killed in a motorcycle accident a little over a month ago."

"Oh, John Lee," she murmured, "I didn't know." She pressed a hand against her heart, remembering the tow-headed little girl who had shadowed her big brother's every step from the time she could walk. "I'm so sorry. You were so close. That must have been horrible for you."

He dipped his chin to his chest and scuffed the toe of his boot at a plank on the front porch. "Yeah, it was, but truthfully I lost Sissy a long time ago." He lifted his gaze to meet hers, his blue eyes a deep pool of grief that Merideth well understood. "You wouldn't have known her, Merideth. After Mom and Dad died, she went crazy. Died her hair purple, pierced everything on her body that could be pierced. When she wasn't living on the streets, she was shacking up with first one guy, then another. I doubt she even knew who fathered the baby." He shook his head regretfully. "I tried to help her, but nothing I did or said seemed to make any difference. It was as if she was determined to self-destruct."

Merideth laid a hand on his arm, her touch light but full of compassion. "I wish I'd known. Maybe I could have done something to help her."

He placed his own hand over hers and squeezed. "Thanks, but nothing you could have done or said would have changed anything. Believe me, I tried it all." He drew her hand from his arm to clasp it between his own. He dropped his gaze to stare at them. "But maybe there is something that you could do for Sissy."

Unsure what she could do now that Sissy was gone, Merideth peered at him quizzically. "What?"

John Lee drew in a deep breath and lifted his gaze, his blue eyes meeting hers. "I need help with Cassie. Mrs. Baker, my housekeeper, takes care of her through the day, but the woman isn't as young as she used to be. And with all her other household chores...well, the baby's not getting the attention she requires. What Cassie needs is a nanny."

Merideth tensed, sensing the direction the conversation was taking. "Is that why you invited me to dinner? To persuade *me* to become the baby's nanny?"

He had the grace to blush. "Well, yeah, sorta."

Her lips thinned and she jerked her hand from his. "Then you wasted your time. Look elsewhere. I'm not interested."

When she turned for the house, John Lee stepped in front of her again. Merideth snapped her head up to glare at him.

"I have looked," he said. "I really have." He dug his hands deep into his jean pockets. "You don't realize how hard it is to find someone competent, someone I'd trust with her. That's why I was hoping you'd be willing to help me out for a while. You wouldn't be her nanny, really. More like her friend."

When her eyes narrowed dangerously, John Lee pressed on. "It'd just be for a couple of months. Just until I can find someone permanent. You told me you didn't know what you wanted to do with your life," he reminded her. "This'll give you something to occupy your time while you're making up your mind. And you can live on the ranch with Cassie and me. That way you won't feel like you're a burden on your sisters anymore. It's the perfect arrangement for everyone. Don't you see?"

Though Merideth's gaze was riveted on John Lee's face, the image she saw was that of Cassie, that beautiful little baby, standing in the playpen, her arms outstretched to Merideth, tears streaking down her red face, that silent plea in her eyes.

Slowly she backed away from him. "No," she said, her voice thick with emotion. "I'm sorry, but I can't." Spinning around she ran from the porch and across the lawn.

* * *

"Why didn't either of you tell me?" Merideth demanded accusingly of her sisters.

Mandy and Sam exchanged a guilty look, but as the oldest and the one who'd ultimately made the decision to keep the news from her, it was Mandy who responded. "I'm sorry, Merideth. I know we should have, but—well, right after Sissy's accident, you had your accident and we didn't think you needed to be burdened with any more bad news."

Merideth folded her arms beneath her breasts. "So you're making my decisions for me now, are you? And I suppose you both were in on this little scheme with John Lee, too, weren't you, thinking I'd go along with his idea? Well, you were wrong!" she cried, flattening her hands on her father's desk as she leaned across it to glare at them. "I won't do it. I can't."

"Whoa, wait a minute," Sam said, rising from the sofa. "What scheme?"

Narrowing her eyes suspiciously, Merideth shifted her gaze from Sam's to Mandy's and back again, looking for signs of guilt, for the lie she was sure that her sisters were trying to brazen out. But she saw nothing there but confusion. "He didn't tell you?"

Sam tossed her hands in the air in frustration. "Tell us, what, for heaven's sake?"

"That he wants me to move in with him and take care of Sissy's baby."

Mandy's eyes widened and she leapt from the sofa. "What! Oh, Merideth, surely you know that we'd never ask you to do something like that. That would be cruel. Your own loss is still much too fresh."

Merideth folded her arms beneath her breasts again and turned her back on her sisters to stare out the darkened window. "Yes, it is," she said, feeling tears rising. "But obviously John Lee doesn't think so."

The days faded one into the other until a week had passed since Merideth's conversation with John Lee. During that week, she had paced her room, walked the pastures of the Double-Cross, driven for miles on end, all the while cursing John Lee Carter.

Why had he done this to her? Didn't he realize how painful it was for her to see someone else's baby when her heart was still raw from the loss of her own?

And that baby. That precious little angel. As hard as she tried, Merideth couldn't shake her image…or the desperation in John Lee's voice when he'd said he needed help with the child.

She tried hard not to feel sorry for him, to hold on to her anger with him, but it was obvious that he was in way over his head. What did a bachelor, especially a playboy like John Lee, know about caring for a baby?

The poor little thing, left without a mother to love and care for her. Merideth tried to blot the infant from her mind, but she couldn't sleep at night for worrying about her, wondering if she was okay, if John Lee had found someone to care for her, if she was receiving the proper care.

After a week of sleepless nights and haunted days, she finally decided she wouldn't rest until she saw the child again and satisfied herself that the baby was receiving the attention and care she needed. She owed Sissy that.

She planned her visit mid-morning in hopes of avoiding John Lee, sure that he would be out on the ranch with his wranglers at that time of day.

Parking in front of the long, ranch-style house, she crossed to the porch and rang the bell. From the other side of the door, she could hear the drone of a television set…and the plaintive cry of the baby. She waited, her nerves winding tighter and tighter with each passing moment, with each new heartbreaking sob.

She punched the bell a second time. Then, unable to stand the sound of the baby's crying, tried the door and found it open. She stepped inside. "Mrs. Baker? John Lee?"

She listened but heard nothing but the baby's persistent cry. Had something happened to the housekeeper? Was the baby alone and in pain? With panic gripping her chest, Merideth ran down the hall, following the crying sounds to the den.

There she found a playpen in the center of the room and inside it Cassie stood on wobbly legs, her fingers knotted in the playpen's mesh sides. She stood just as she had the last time Merideth had seen her. Dressed in nothing but a fruit-stained T-shirt and a sagging diaper, she turned her face toward Merideth. Alligator-sized tears ran down her face.

Merideth glanced frantically around, looking for some sign of John Lee or Mrs. Baker, hoping they would hear the baby's cries and would come and see to her needs. But no one came. There wasn't a sound in the house other than that of canned laughter from a television set in another room. Merideth swallowed the fear that rose as she turned her gaze back to Cassie.

Tears burned her throat. She'd made a mistake, she told herself. She shouldn't have come. She couldn't bear this.

She started to turn away, to leave before anyone saw her, but just as she did, the baby swayed, losing her balance, then sat down hard on the floor of the playpen. Her frustrated wails grew louder.

Instinctively, Merideth took a step toward her, her hands outstretched, reaching for her…then she stopped, curling her hands into fists against her lips. She couldn't pick her up. She couldn't touch her. She just couldn't.

As if Cassie sensed Merideth's inability to rescue her, she flopped over on her tummy and buried her face in the blanket beneath her, sobbing miserably.

Swallowing hard, Merideth quickly closed the distance between them and stooped to pick her up. Cassie grabbed at Merideth's hair, tangling the fingers of one hand there, while she fisted her other hand in Merideth's blouse. Straightening, Merideth held her out in front of her.

Emotion rose in her throat as she met the infant's gaze. "Shhh," she whispered, blinded by her own tears. "Please don't cry." But Cassie only wailed louder. With her heart threatening to split wide open, Merideth drew a deep breath and slowly drew her to her breasts. The frantic beat of the baby's heart throbbed against her own.

She closed her eyes, trying to remain unaffected, but the baby's warmth seeped through her blouse and slowly wound itself around her heart. Merideth couldn't hold back the tide of grief that rose inside her.

Cupping the back of the baby's head, she tucked it beneath her chin and pressed her lips to the cap of silky hair there. Inhaling deeply, she filled her senses with scents of baby powder, milk and innocence.

"There, there," she soothed as she instinctively began to sway. "No need to cry. Merideth's got you."

A hiccupy sigh reverberated against Merideth's chest, then Cassie leaned back and looked up at her. Tears swam in eyes as blue as John Lee's. She peered up at Merideth innocently, yet with a look of such expectancy and hopefulness, that Merideth felt as if the child had reached in and touched her heart.

Tears blurred her vision as she tried to focus on the baby's sweet face. How could she have ever been so heartless, she asked herself, so selfish as to run from this precious child?

"What's the matter, sweetheart?" she murmured sympathetically as she swiped tears from her own eyes. "Are you wet? Do you need your diaper changed?" In answer, Cassie's lower lip began to quiver. Merideth tested the diaper. "You are wet," she confirmed. "And I'll bet you're hungry, too." She glanced around. "Where is Mrs. Baker?" she asked, beginning to frown. "She should be taking care of you."

"*C,* you fool. Ask for a *C!*"

Merideth turned toward the sound and anger slowly rose to warm her cheeks. "The irresponsible twit," she muttered to the baby. "Watching television and leaving you alone in here and all by yourself." Furious now, she marched in the direction of the swinging door that separated the kitchen from the den. Slapping a palm against it, she stepped into the kitchen, then stopped, shifting Cassie to her hip while the door rocked on its hinges behind her.

Just as she'd expected, she found Mrs. Baker standing at the kitchen's center island, her hands white with flour, her eyes glued to a television set on the counter opposite her. Pursing her lips, Merideth marched across the room and with an angry stab of her finger, punched the power button. The screen went black, the room silent.

Mrs. Baker turned from the screen to Merideth, her eyes widening in surprise when she saw Meredith, obviously unaware of her presence before that moment. "What do you think you're doing?" she blustered indignantly.

"Turning off the television."

Mrs. Baker narrowed her eyes suspiciously, shifting her gaze from Merideth to the baby and back again. "How did you get in here?"

Cassie started to cry again and Merideth bounced her on her hip, trying to quiet her. "I walked right in the front door, the same as any kidnapper or murderer could do."

Her expression turning sour, the housekeeper gathered her apron in her hands and wiped the flour from them. "And what gives you the right to march into a private home unannounced?"

"I rang the bell twice, but you were so engrossed in Vanna White flipping letters," she said with a dramatic wave of her hand toward the television set, "that I guess you didn't hear."

"An unlocked door gives you no right to just barge in." She shook a finger at Merideth. "John Lee'll hear about this, I assure you."

"No need. I'll tell him myself. And while I'm at it, I'll tell him how you were watching television and ignoring the baby's needs."

Mrs. Baker's mouth dropped open. "I was *not* ignoring the baby!"

"You most certainly were! She was in the den crying her heart out. I could hear the poor thing all the way from the front porch."

At that moment, the back door swung open, and John Lee stepped into the kitchen. In the midst of dragging off his hat, he froze when he saw Merideth holding the baby.

"What are you doing here?" he asked in surprise as he tossed his hat onto the counter top.

"That's exactly what *I* was trying to get out of her." Mrs. Baker huffed and shot an accusing look at Merideth.

Ignoring her, Merideth turned on John Lee, having to

raise her voice to be heard over Cassie's crying. "This woman is totally irresponsible. When I arrived, Cassie was in the den in her playpen screaming her lungs out while *she*—" she pointed an accusing finger at Mrs. Baker "—was watching TV in the kitchen. She is incompetent and lazy and I want her fired immediately!"

Seeing the color rise on his housekeeper's face, John Lee quickly crossed the room and took Merideth by the elbow. "Excuse us for a minute, Mrs. Baker," he said apologetically, as he propelled Merideth toward the swinging door. "I'll take care of this."

Merideth dug in her heels, but John Lee shoved her kicking and fussing ahead of him. Once in the den, he spun her around to face him. "What in the hell do you think you're doing?" he whispered angrily. "Do you realize how hard it is to get good help these days?"

"Good help!" Merideth cried. "Why, that woman—"

John Lee clamped a hand over her mouth. "Don't you say another word," he threatened. "I'll be lucky if she doesn't quit over this."

Merideth ripped his hand from her mouth. "You'll be lucky if she *does* quit!" she returned furiously.

Firming his lips, John Lee caught her by the elbow again and marched her down the hall to the master bedroom. Once inside, he slammed the door behind him and fisted his hands on his hips. "Let me tell you something, Miss High-and-Mighty McCloud. I *need* Mrs. Baker. Without her help with Cassie, I don't know what I'd do."

Merideth shifted the baby to her shoulder and frantically patted her back, trying to calm her. "You'd find someone better. Someone conscientious. Someone without a television addiction."

Shooting Merideth a scathing look, John Lee took the baby from her. Holding Cassie at arm's length, he jounced her up and down, puckering his mouth sympathetically as he looked up at her. "Whatsa matter, darlin'? Is all this yellin' upsettin' you?"

Merideth snatched the baby right back from him. "For heaven's sake! She isn't some football you can toss around." She cradled the baby to her chest, tucking the infant's head beneath her chin and rocking slightly while she glared at John Lee. "And I can tell you what's wrong with her. She's wet. She's dirty. And probably hungry. And that witch in the kitchen totally ignores her."

John Lee narrowed his eyes. "Don't you start in again with me," he warned.

"As if anything I said could penetrate your thick skull." Turning her back on him, Merideth paced the room, patting and comforting, trying to calm Cassie. A huge beveled mirror covered the wall opposite her from floor to ceiling, offering Merideth her reflection and that of the black velvet comforter and cowhide throw that stretched across the king-sized bed behind her. She knew without looking that she'd find a similar mirror on the ceiling. She also knew their purpose. She shifted her gaze to a huge impressionistic painting of bold red slashes. After staring at it a moment, she realized she was looking at a nude woman's reclining form.

The entire room screamed of seduction.

She glanced over her shoulder to scowl at John Lee. "I suppose this is *your* room?"

"Yeah," he said defensively. "You got a problem with that?"

"Yes, I do, though I imagine the caliber of women you entertain here probably find this hedonistic display highly erotic."

John Lee wasn't at all sure what she'd just said, but

by her tone, he figured he'd just been insulted. "I'll have you know—"

Merideth shifted Cassie to the opposite shoulder, cutting him off with a dismissing wave of her hand. "Don't bother me with the details of your sordid sex life. Just tell me where the baby's room is so that I can change her."

Scowling, John Lee gestured toward a door. "Through here."

Merideth followed him into the adjoining room, which proved to be an extension of the den of iniquity she considered his bedroom. An entertainment center lined one wall and a sleek black leather couch, deep enough to sleep on, another. Framed photographs hung above the sofa and Merideth focused in on the largest, a picture of John Lee surrounded by a group of big-busted cheerleaders, each of whom seemed intent on offering him the most daring view of her cleavage. By the broad smile he was wearing, Merideth could tell he had been enjoying himself immensely.

"Disgusting," she muttered under her breath and brushed past John Lee, heading for the crib parked in a corner of the room.

She laid the baby down, her expression and her tone softening perceptibly as she turned her full attention on Cassie. "That's okay, precious," she soothed, drawing a clean diaper from the bag hanging on the side of the crib. "Merideth will take care of that old wet diaper."

As she worked, the trio of gold bangles at her wrist clinked musically. Mesmerized by the sound, Cassie stopped crying and stretched up a chubby hand to grab for them. Laughing, Merideth slipped one off her wrist and gave it her. "You like jewelry, do you? Well, so do I. And I must say you have marvelous taste." When Cassie carried the bracelet to her mouth and began to gum it, Merideth smiled approvingly. "That's right, darling. It's only fitting that a princess should cut her teeth on gold."

John Lee wasn't sure what to make of all this, but damned if he was going to say or do anything to stop it! Merideth was holding Cassie, talking to her, even teasing her. This from the woman who, a little more than a week ago, couldn't bring herself to so much as touch the baby.

Was it possible that she had reconsidered his proposal?

Cautiously, he eased up behind Merideth and peered over her shoulder as she pressed the tabs of the clean diaper in place. "You're pretty good at that."

Merideth favored him with a look that would have brought a lesser man to his knees. "Any fool can change a diaper, which only supports my claim that Mrs. Baker is incompetent. You should fire her."

John Lee cocked his head in warning. "Merideth…"

"Oh, forget it." She glanced around. "Where do you keep her clothes? You *do* have something other than these tacky T-shirts for her to wear, don't you?"

"Of course I do." He dug through a box of clothes sitting on the floor beside the crib, and pulled out a pink romper and held it up for her inspection. "Will this do?"

Merideth eyed it critically. "For now." She took the garment and tugged it over Cassie's head. "We'll go shopping later."

"Shopping?"

"Yes, shopping."

"For what?"

"A new wardrobe." She bent to lift Cassie from the crib and shifted her to her hip. "She'll need furniture, too. A chest of drawers, a changing table and a rocker, of course." She crossed to the window and opened the shutters, letting sunlight flood the room. Turning, she cocked her head, studying the walls, already mentally ripping the pictures from them. "And paint," she added thoughtfully.

"Paint?" John Lee repeated, wondering what in the hell was going on, but afraid to ask.

"Yes. This room is much too dull. A baby needs color for stimulation. We'll need to drive into Austin, and maybe even to San Antonio."

"And when are we going to do this?"

"First thing in the morning. We'd go today," she added, already thinking of fabrics and colors, "but I need to go home and pack a few things."

"Pack a few things?" he repeated, beginning to feel like a parrot. "Are you planning on moving in?"

Merideth rolled her eyes. "Well, of course I am. Someone has to look after Cassie, and it's obvious *she*—" she jerked her head toward the kitchen "—isn't capable of the job. And *you*," she added pointedly, "are too spineless to fire her." She turned to Cassie, nuzzling her nose against the infant's. "Isn't that right, princess?"

In answer, Cassie caught Merideth's cheeks between her chubby hands and pressed their noses closer together.

Laughing, Merideth gave her a quick hug before turning to John Lee. When her gaze met his, her frown returned.

"I suppose we should get a few details out of the way," she said, her tone turning crisp. "I'll take care of Cassie, but that's it. I do not cook, clean or do laundry, including my own. I'll sleep in your room, so that I can be nearby in case she cries out in the night, which of course means that you'll need to move into one of the other bedrooms."

Though the idea of giving up his room didn't exactly

please John Lee, he figured he could live with the incon-
venience for a few months if it meant Merideth was going
to be looking after Cassie. "Sounds fair enough. What
else?"

"You'll need to provide me with transportation, as I
don't own a car. I'm sure—"

John Lee's eyes bugged out. "You don't own a car?"

Merideth lifted a negligent shoulder. "In New York I
never had need of one. The studio provided me with a
chauffeured limousine."

He could see her sliding into the back of a stretch limo
and giving a driver orders in that snooty way of hers. The
image suited her. But he figured he better let her know
up front that she wasn't in New York anymore where
everyone danced to whatever tune she played. *Or* at the
Double-Cross, where everyone spoiled her unmercifully.

"Well, sugar, I hate to tell you this," he said sadly,
"but there isn't a limousine on the place. You'll just have
to use one of the farm trucks."

Merideth crossed to him and patted his cheek, smiling
sweetly. "Why, thank you, John Lee, for your generosity,
but frankly I prefer the Porsche."

Three

Scowling, John Lee trailed Merideth to the house loaded down with four shopping bags and a huge box containing, of all things, a life-size Raggedy Ann doll. He'd already made two trips, and it looked as if he'd be making at least two more before he'd transferred all Merideth's purchases to the nursery.

The very thought made his knee throb in protest.

"Hurry up, John Lee," Merideth called over her shoulder. "I want to get started on Cassie's room as soon as possible."

"Hurry up, John Lee," he mocked, limping along behind her. "If you're in such an all-fired hurry," he grumped, "then why don't you carry some of this crap?"

Merideth stopped and turned to look at him. "Because I have the baby." Smiling sweetly, she pivoted and continued up the steps.

John Lee frowned at her back. "Why don't I get to carry the baby?"

"Because that's my job," she reminded him. She opened the door, then shifted the sleeping Cassie to cradle her in her opposite arm so she could prop the door open with her hip. "Besides," she added, batting her eyelashes flirtatiously, "carrying those little old bags should be a snap for someone as big and strong as you."

With a snort, John Lee pushed past her. "Save your breath," he muttered. "I know you too well to be suckered by your sweet talk."

Merideth let the door close behind her. "You consider that sweet talk?" she teased, as she followed him. "Darling, you don't even know what sweet talk is."

"And I don't want to know," he grumbled. He picked his way through the minefield of suitcases Merideth had dumped in his bedroom earlier that morning, then squeezed through the door connecting the bedroom to his den. After dropping the packages to the floor, he flexed his fingers, trying to get the blood running through them again. "The rest of that stuff can wait."

"But, John Lee—"

"No buts," he warned, wagging a finger beneath her nose. "If you want the rest of it in here, you can haul it. I'm done." Having had his say, he turned and stalked from the room.

Merideth smothered a laugh. "That's what he thinks," she whispered to the sleeping Cassie as she tucked her into her crib for the rest of her nap. She waited a moment, to make sure she'd settled, then tiptoed to the door and closed it softly behind her. When she turned, she found John Lee sprawled on his back on the king-size bed, his arms flung wide.

"Excuse me, but I think you're on my bed."

John Lee groaned. "Have a heart, Merideth. It was the closest one."

Still high from the day of shopping, she sat down beside him. "What's wrong, John Lee?" she teased, giving his cheek a playful pat. "Did we wear you out?"

He growled and batted her hand away.

Chuckling softly, she kicked off her shoes and leaned back, supporting herself with her elbows. Tipping her head to one side, she wiggled her toes and admired her nail polish. "You know," she said thoughtfully, "shopping is a lot like sex."

John Lee cracked open one eye to peer at her. "In what way?"

"Afterwards, a woman is energized and ready for more, while all a man wants to do is sleep."

In spite of his weariness, John Lee chuckled. "I'll agree on the shopping part, but as to sex…well, I'd have to say that depends on the man."

"Oh, really?" she challenged, cocking her head to look at him. "And I suppose you're the exception to the rule?"

Smiling smugly, he laced his fingers across his chest. "Sugar, where sex is involved, I'm the exception to every rule."

She snorted. "Egotist."

"No, I just know my strengths." He rolled his head to the side and grinned up at her. "Want me to prove it?"

"Do you want *me* to break your nose?" she returned.

He chuckled. "And ruin this pretty face?"

Rolling her eyes, Merideth lay back, settling beside him, then groaned when her gaze met her reflection on the ceiling. "That is sick," she said, frowning at the mirror above.

John Lee stifled a yawn. "What's sick?"

"*That!*"

He opened his eyes and met her gaze in the mirror above them. They lay side by side, their shoulders almost touching.

"And that, too," she added, pointing to the mirrored wall beside the bed.

His mouth curved in a teasing grin when her gaze met his again on the ceiling. "I don't know. Personally, I kind of like 'em."

"You would," she grumbled. She snagged the corner of the pillow beneath his head, gave it a tug and plopped her head down on it. "This room looks like something straight out of a cathouse."

"You ever been in a cathouse?"

Merideth squirmed, nudging him over, until she had the lion's share of the pillow. "No, but I played a call girl once."

"A call girl, huh?"

Comfortable now, she met his gaze in the mirror. "Yes, a call girl. A very expensive one, I might add."

"Were you any good?"

She smiled smugly. "The best."

Wide awake now, John Lee rolled to his side, propping an elbow on the mattress and his cheek on his palm as he looked at her. It wasn't a stretch to imagine Merideth playing the part of a high-priced prostitute. With those pouty lips, that voluptuous figure and those sultry eyes, she would be a natural for the part.

A woman like her could drive a man wild...and did, he was sure.

Of course, she'd had years of practice to prepare for the part. Even as a teenager she'd been aware of her feminine wiles and had honed them to a razor-sharp edge on her unsuspecting male classmates. Fights were fought over her, bets made and lost as to who would win her heart. But even though she'd had her pick of the guys, he couldn't remember her ever having a steady boyfriend. He supposed it was because she'd enjoyed all the attention too much to sacrifice it for the love of just one man.

Three years her senior, John Lee had never competed with the others for her attention. He'd never needed to. He'd had his hands full keeping all the girls who'd chased after him satisfied. But he'd been aware of her, just the same.

Any other woman undergoing as close a scrutiny as John Lee was giving her right now might have fidgeted and fussed, but not Merideth. She was way too sure of herself to squirm. She met his gaze squarely, confidently and maybe a bit cockily.

"The best, huh?" he said, eyeing her.

"The *very* best."

"What was your specialty?"

She laughed at his question, that low sultry laugh of hers that crawled along a man's nerves and tightened his groin.

"I wasn't the star in some porno flick, if that's what you're thinking," she told him. "It was daytime television. In fact, as I recall, there was actually only one scene with a john. Monique, the character I play, or rather played," she amended, frowning as she remembered that the part was no longer hers. Marcus had stripped her of it, just before— She stanched the thought before it could fully form, not wanting to think about the past and all she'd lost. "Anyway," she went on, "Monique had a dual personality that surfaced from time to time. She was the wife of a successful doctor, and her alter ego, Charise, was the prostitute. Unfortunately—"

While she rattled on with her synopsis of the story line and the description of her character, John Lee only half listened, his attention stolen by the movement of her lips.

She had a delectable mouth. Full and soft, the points of her upper lip's bow sharp and well-defined. He wondered what those lips would feel like pressed against his, moving in a slow sensual mating of taste and texture. As he watched, mesmerized, her lips parted and her tongue slipped out to trace a line along her upper lip, wetting it. Her tongue bumped that little tight bow at the center of her upper lip and John Lee had to bite back a groan.

He knew it was a mistake, knew that he might very well be jeopardizing the arrangement that he'd made with Merideth to look after Cassie, but even knowing this, he couldn't resist the temptation to taste her.

Throwing a leg over hers, he hooked his knee behind her thighs and drew her to her side and closer to him. Instinctively, her hands went to his chest and braced there. "John Lee! What are you—"

But before she could fully form the question, he closed his mouth over hers. Satin, he thought, cool, soft satin and a taste as sweet as any he could have imagined. He traced the shape of her lips with his tongue, warming them, then flicked its pointed tip at the bow, teasing her lips apart.

"John Lee!"

His name came to him on a rush of warm, moist air that sent heat shooting through him. "Yeah, sugar?" he whispered as he flattened a hand on her butt and curled himself around her.

"What are you doing?"

"Tasting you." To prove it, he raked his fingers through her hair and knotted them to draw her face to his. The movement brought his arm across her body and his elbow grazed her breast. She sucked in a shocked breath at the intimate contact, her lips parted beneath his. Always a man to take an advantage of an opportunity, John Lee slid his tongue in the opening. He smoothed it across her teeth, then probed deeper, sweeping across the velvet surface of her tongue, then higher to tease the roof of her mouth. He felt her fingers curl into fists against his chest and felt the quickening of her breath in the rapid rise and fall of her breasts beneath his arm.

He smiled against her lips. Yeah, she could drive a man wild, all right. He was beginning to feel a little bit crazy himself.

When he shifted to deepen the kiss, she shifted too, drawing her knee up intimately against his crotch. He groaned against her mouth, finding the pressure unbelievably erotic.

"John Lee?" she whispered, her voice a low seductive purr.

"Yeah, sugar?"

"Can you feel that?" she asked and rubbed her knee suggestively against him.

"Oh, yeah, baby," he replied huskily. "That feels good."

"I'm glad," she said, her voice as smooth as silk, "because you're fixing to feel it in your throat."

He grunted when her knee connected soundly with his crotch, and reared back to look at her in surprise. Blue eyes blazed, piercing his.

Angrily she shoved at his chest. "Get off of me," she demanded through gritted teeth.

Not sure what he'd done to upset her, but knowing her well enough to know that she wouldn't hesitate to make good her threat, John Lee untangled his fingers from her hair and his legs from around her body, keeping his movements slow and careful.

When he rolled away from her, she jackknifed to a sitting position and jerked her blouse back into place. Twisting at the waist, she glared at him. "Taste me!" she all but spat at him. "As if I'm some morsel of food to be savored." Her eyes narrowed dangerously, she rolled to her knees, planting her hands on the mattress between them.

"For your information, I am *not* one of those bimbos whose pictures you've hung on the wall in your den like some kind of sexual trophies. I—"

"Now wait just a damn minute," he began defensively, "those women—"

"You don't have to tell me about *those* women," Merideth replied scathingly. "I know the type. Groupies who'd drop their pom-poms in a heartbeat for a chance to hop into bed with you or one of your studly friends." She rose to her knees, her breasts heaving, her eyes wild as she glared down at him. "They may enjoy your kinky mirrors," she said, flinging a hand in the direction of the ceiling, "and they may get some kind of orgasmic thrill from being pawed by you, but *I* don't!"

"Pawed?" John Lee repeated, pushing himself to an elbow.

"Yes, pawed!" She scooted off the bed and stood, her hands braced at her hips. "And if you think that I'm going to spend the next several months dodging your passes, you've got another think coming."

Where he was confused before, now John Lee was mad. Damn mad. No one challenged his prowess as a lover. No one. Not even Merideth McCloud. He rolled off the bed and to his feet.

Merideth knew he was angry, could see it in his eyes,

in the set of his jaw. Never was she more aware of his size or his strength, than at that moment. Yet, it was neither of those things that frightened her. It was his voice. When he spoke it was with a deathly calm.

"I don't know what kind of men you've dealt with in the past," he said as he took a menacing step toward her. "And I don't know how they go about showing a woman they find her attractive, nor what they call it when they do." He took another step and Merideth found herself backed up against the wall.

Bracing a hand at either side of her head, he leaned over her, pushing his face up close to hers. "But, sugar, where I come from, when a man is attracted to a woman, he lets her know by kissing her." Before Merideth could stop him, he'd closed his mouth over hers and thrust his tongue deeply into her mouth.

The capture was so complete, so unexpected, she felt her knees weaken, her heart slam against her ribs.

"And sometimes even touching her," he murmured against her mouth. To demonstrate, he slipped a hand between them and smoothed his palm across her breast.

Though she stiffened, willing herself not to respond, the heat, the friction of his hand burned through her, and her nipple hardened beneath his palm and began to ache.

He drew his head back just far enough to meet her eyes. "You Yankees might call it pawing," he said, his eyes burning into hers, "but down here in Texas, we call it foreplay." With his gaze still locked on hers, he withdrew his hand. She closed her eyes and dragged in a shuddering breath, then opened them to find him still watching her.

"But don't you worry that pretty little head of yours about me making any more passes at you," he told her.

He pushed away from the wall and from her. "I prefer my women willing and warm."

"Willing and warm," Merideth muttered viciously. Rearing back, she threw an armload of shoes into the closet, then kicked the door closed behind them. "As if I'm not."

She whipped the skirt of her robe aside to keep it from tangling around her bare legs as she whirled for the bed. With a disregard for the delicate fabrics scattered there, she raked her clothes to the floor, then flopped down on her back and flung her arms wide.

The mirror above her offered a full view of the king-size bed with its padded headboard of black-and-white cowhide, its yards of downy black satin and its cowhide throw. If ever a room deserved the tag "love nest," this one did. She could almost see John Lee rolling around beneath the mirror with one of his bimbos, naked, his body slick with perspiration.

"Pervert," she muttered, and turned to her stomach and away from the upsetting image.

Fisting her hands beneath her chin, she stared at her reflection on the opposite wall, still angry with John Lee for suggesting she was frigid. She wasn't frigid, she told herself. She just didn't like surprises, that was all, and John Lee had definitely caught her off guard when he'd made that pass at her. She liked control, felt safe with it, and didn't like it when someone snatched it from her hands. And John Lee had definitely done that.

She groaned and dropped her head, pressing her forehead against her fists, remembering the shock she'd felt when he'd first wrapped his leg around her and pulled her to him. Before she could even take a breath, his mouth had covered hers, drawing her in, stripping her bare of her defenses.

Yes, his kiss had been devastating, his touch electrifying...but she hadn't been expecting it, hadn't been prepared for the depth of her response. So she'd struck out at him, clawing at him, fighting for the control that she'd lost and so desperately needed.

She'd overreacted, and, in doing so, made a fool of herself. A big bumbling fool.

Groaning, she lifted her face and propped her chin on her fists again to stare miserably at her reflection. She didn't like looking like a fool, any more than she liked losing control. But what could she do about it now?

She supposed she could apologize, explain to John Lee that her response to him was simply a reflexive action, a defense mechanism. But if she apologized, then that would be the same as admitting that she'd done something wrong, that she'd made a mistake, and that didn't sit well with Merideth, either. Especially since John Lee had insulted her by insinuating that she was frigid.

Frigid. Hah! She was anything but frigid. Her body's response to his first kiss was proof enough of that. But of course he didn't know he'd made her toes curl, her heart nearly jump out of her chest. All he'd seen was her anger.

And that second kiss! A shiver chased down her spine as she remembered the heat in it, the feel of his hand on her breast, her nipple budding beneath it.

He'd said he was attracted to her—she distinctly remembered him telling her so—and that his actions were a result of that attraction. He'd even gone so far as to label them foreplay.

Foreplay. The word itself was seductive, suggestive and when demonstrated by John Lee, devastating—which in itself was a surprise. In all the years she'd known John Lee, she'd never considered him romantically. He was simply a friend, nothing more. But now she was forced to reconsider.

She cocked her head and studied her reflection thoughtfully. Given the proper setting, the right mood, she might actually enjoy pursuing that "attraction," as he'd called it, and experiencing a little more of his unique brand of foreplay.

But don't you worry that pretty little head of yours about me making any more passes at you. I prefer my women willing and warm.

She frowned, her fists tightening beneath her chin as his last words came to mind. Darn it! She *wanted* him to make another pass at her.

But he wouldn't. Not after the scene she'd made.

She narrowed her eyes as she considered the situation. She'd just have to prove to him that she was warm and willing, she decided. Of course, she couldn't make the first move. Her pride simply wouldn't let her. But she knew how to draw a man's attention. She knew how to flirt. In no time at all, she'd have him panting after her, begging to kiss her again.

Pleased with herself and her plan, she rose from the bed, feeling energized. Picking up the clothes she'd strewn on the floor, she tossed them on the bed and began to fold them. A cry from the other room had her dropping them again.

Cassie had awakened from her nap.

"Coming, darling," she sang cheerfully as she all but sailed for the nursery door.

Merideth heard the kitchen door swing open behind her and glanced over her shoulder. "Good morning, John

Lee,'' she said in greeting.

He froze at the sight of her, his eyes going wide. Merideth lifted a hand, pressing her fingertips into the bare cleavage her nightgown left exposed between her breasts, intentionally drawing his gaze there. ''I'm sorry,'' she said, all wide-eyed innocence. ''I didn't realize you were up. If I'd known, I would've thrown on a robe.''

It was a lie, of course. She'd planned her early-morning visit to the kitchen on purpose, hoping to bump into John Lee before he left for the day. She'd chosen her nightgown with the same goal in mind.

Designed for seduction, the gown's fabric was sheer, but not transparent, merely hinting at the curves beneath. Lace panels, no more than four inches in width, stretched in soft gathers from the gown's empire waist from front to back, were all that covered her breasts.

She watched John Lee's Adam's apple bob convulsively, his hands clench at his sides, and silently applauded herself. Yes, she definitely knew how to grab a man's attention.

''Can I get you a cup of coffee?'' she asked, cocking her head in question. When he didn't answer, but continued to stare at her breasts, she took a step toward him. ''John Lee?''

His head snapped up, his gaze hitting•hers. ''What?''

She smiled sweetly, innocently. ''I asked if you would like a cup of coffee.''

He swallowed again, and Merideth could tell it was an effort for him to keep his gaze from dropping to her breasts again. ''N-no,'' he stammered. ''I don't have time.''

''Oh?'' She sidled closer, her nightgown whispering

around her legs. "And where are you off to so early this morning?"

"I—I—" He cleared his throat. "I've got to drive into Austin and pick up a tractor part."

She reached up and brushed an imaginary piece of lint from his shirtfront. His body jerked spasmodically at her touch and Merideth had to bite back a smug smile.

"You be careful, now, you hear?" she told him, her voice dripping honey. "That traffic can be beastly at this hour." Giving his cheek an affectionate pat, she puckered her lips and blew him a kiss, then swept past him and through the swinging door.

John Lee dumped the box of parts on the workbench in the barn and glanced around, looking for Bill, his foreman and sometime mechanic.

"Bill!" he yelled, anxious to get the part in place and the tractor back out in the hay field. He waited, listening, but the only sound that came to him was the purr of the barn cat that was currently wrapping itself around his legs.

He gave the cat an impatient nudge with his foot. "Where is everybody?" he muttered irritably as he strode from the barn. Once outside, he stopped and looked around, expecting to at least find his wranglers about their chores. But he didn't see a soul, which slapped a thick coat of icing on an already lousy cake of a day.

It had all started earlier that morning in the kitchen when he'd bumped into Merideth wearing that bit of nothing. Hell, he admitted silently, his bad mood had started before then. It had begun the evening before when she'd gone ballistic on him, and all over an innocent little kiss. The way she'd carried on, a person would think he'd tried to assault her or something, when all he'd done and intended to do, was taste her. She'd aroused his curiosity and he'd just wanted to ease it, nothing more.

Oh, and he'd tasted her, all right, he remembered as he headed for the house. But he hadn't come close to satisfying his curiosity. If anything, he'd given himself more to wonder about, to fantasize over. Like what it would be like to peel off her clothes real slow, and what her skin would feel like bare, rubbing against his.

Just thinking about it made his pulse kick, his groin tighten. Angry with himself for even giving her a second thought, he yanked open the kitchen door.

At the sound, Mrs. Baker turned from the stove, a wooden spoon dripping in her hand.

"Have you seen Bill?" he asked irritably. "His truck's out by the barn, but I can't find him anywhere."

With a sniff, Mrs. Baker tipped up her chin and went back to her stirring. "That woman has him."

"Merideth?"

She lifted the spoon and whacked it against the side of the pan, sending juice flying, her disapproval of Merideth obvious. "Him and a few others, as well. Has them all dancing to her tune. Mark my words," she said, turning to shake the spoon at John Lee. "You'll rue the day you brought her here. She'll be the ruination of 'em all before its over."

John Lee pressed his finger and thumb on the bridge of his nose and squeezed. He didn't need this right now. He knew Mrs. Baker didn't like Merideth. She'd already made her position on that crystal clear.

He heaved a deep breath. "Where are they?" he asked, dropping his hand.

She flung an arm in the direction of the swinging door.

"Back yonder. Has 'em tearing the place apart. Told 'em their other chores could wait."

John Lee's temper soared at the news. "Oh, she did, did she?" Setting his jaw, he ripped off his hat and sent it sailing toward the counter where it hit a pie pan and landed with a clatter. "Well, we'll just see about that."

Marching across the room, he hit the swinging door with the flat of his hand and sent it rocking back on its hinges. As he passed through the den, he heard the murmur of male voices and the husky sound of Merideth's laughter, and his anger climbed a notch higher.

Pulling his men from their jobs, he fumed silently. She probably had them lugging her suitcases for her and helping her unpack. Spoiled little brat. Well, he'd set her straight real quick. His men were wranglers, not lady's maids.

When he reached the master bedroom, he found Bill, his foreman, standing on a ladder at one corner of the room, holding a wire in his hand, while Rudy, one of his wranglers, was perched similarly in the opposite corner, holding the other end. The remainder of the wire was hidden behind the mirror that covered the wall. Dumbfounded, John Lee watched while the two men sawed the wire back and forth, their faces reddening with the effort.

"What in Sam Hill is going on in here?" he roared.

Bill jumped, nearly losing his footing, and grabbed for the top of the ladder to keep from falling. The red in his face deepened when he saw John Lee. "Uh, hi, boss."

John Lee took another step into the room. "What in the hell do you think you're doing?"

"Well, me and Rudy here," Bill explained, gesturing to the man on the other ladder, "was trying to bring down this mirror for Miss Merideth."

At that moment, the woman in question breezed through the open nursery door. Dressed in khaki shorts that barely covered her butt and a peach-colored tank top that hugged her breasts like a second skin, she beamed at John Lee.

"Hi," she greeted him cheerfully. "I thought I heard your voice." She turned her smile on Bill and batted those big baby blues. "Would you do an itsy-bitsy favor for me?"

Bill was scrambling down the ladder, tripping all over himself in his haste to help her. And no wonder, John Lee thought angrily. A woman like Merideth, especially dressed as she was, was hard to say no to when she turned on the charm.

He stuck out a hand, planting it against Bill's chest, stopping him. "Two seconds, Merideth," he said angrily, glaring at her. "That's all the time I'm giving you to explain what the hell's going on here."

She spread her arms wide, her smiling broadening. "We're decorating the nursery." She quickly stepped to the side to make way for the leather couch that appeared in the doorway behind her, carried by two of the other wranglers.

"Excuse me, boss," Joe murmured as he squeezed past John Lee.

Billy, who supported the other end, merely nodded a bashful greeting as he passed by.

Speechless, John Lee watched the men disappear with his couch. It was a full second before he could move, but when he did, he was barreling across the room, headed for what he once considered his private domain. He braced his hands against the door frame to peer inside.

The couch where he liked to kick back with a cold beer and watch old game videos on the giant screen TV wasn't the only item he found missing. The TV was gone, too, as was the entertainment center that usually held it. Walls that had once been covered with pictures and trophy-laden shelves attesting to his successful career as a star quarterback were stripped bare.

Gone. All of it gone. All the things he'd collected over the years. All the furniture and electronic equipment he'd selected with such painstaking care for the sole purpose of his own pleasure and entertainment. The only items left in the room were Cassie's crib and the box that held her clothes.

Merideth strolled past him, paint samples fanned in front of her face. "I'm thinking a pale yellow," she said, cocking her head first to one side then the other as she eyed them critically. "What do you think?"

It was all John Lee could do to keep from closing his hands around her throat and strangling her. "Where is my stuff?"

"In the garage," she replied absently as she angled the samples toward the sunshine streaming through the bare window for a better look. "I'll make arrangements to have it put in storage later."

"Like hell you will!"

Surprised by his angry tone, Merideth turned to look at him. "Excuse me?"

"I want my stuff put back exactly where you found it and I mean *now*."

Merideth inclined her head, her forehead furrowed in confusion. "But I thought this was to be Cassie's nursery?"

"It is."

"But you can't keep your things in here, too," she argued. "There's simply not room."

"The hell I can't."

At his obstinate tone, she folded her arms across her

breasts, and looked at him, her disapproval obvious. "Surely you don't expect Cassie to continue to live out of a box and to sleep with her crib shoved into a corner just so that you can keep all your little toys nearby?"

"She doesn't seem to mind," he replied. "Far as I can tell, she's been getting along just fine with our current arrangement."

"While you have every comfort and every luxury imaginable," Merideth reminded him pointedly. "A king-size bed and dresser, a walk-in closet, a private bath."

Though he tried to dodge them, the implications of his selfishness hit him square in the chest. He shifted uncomfortably, and finally stuck his hands deep into his pockets. "Like I said," he mumbled, "she doesn't seem to mind."

Merideth cocked her head to peer at him, her gaze turning skeptical. "This isn't a temporary arrangement, is it? I mean, you *do* intend to keep Cassie and raise her as your own, don't you?"

"Well, of course I do!" he blustered indignantly. "What would make you ask a crazy thing like that?"

She shrugged and unfolded her arms to put the paint samples in her pocket. "Because Cassie's presence here seems so...so temporary," she finished futilely. She gestured around the room. "A cardboard box for her clothes. A hand-me-down crib. Is this how you intend to provide for her?"

As he looked at each of the items, he realized how meager they looked, how pathetic, especially now that his furniture and equipment was no longer there to disguise their crudeness. The guilt ate a little deeper into his chest.

But it wasn't as if he'd chosen them for her, he told himself defensively. The box holding the baby's clothes was the one Sissy had brought with her when she'd shown up with Cassie in tow, and the crib—a cast-off from one of his friend's kids—had been drafted into service when Sissy had taken off, leaving Cassie behind.

But Merideth was right, he admitted grudgingly. Cassie deserved better. But damned if he could bring himself to admit it to her. He rammed his hands deeper into his pockets, and set his jaw. "She's a baby," he muttered. "What does she care what she sleeps in or where?"

To his surprise, instead of berating him further, Merideth crossed to stand beside him and slipped her arm through his. Her touch was light, but heat curled through him at the contact.

"Oh, John Lee," she murmured in a voice soft with compassion. "Just think of all the changes Cassie's had to adjust to in her short life. Judging from what you've told me, she's never known a real home, not with Sissy moving around all the time. Then to lose her mother, the only constant in her life."

She sighed and leaned against him, resting her head against his arm. "Imagine how terrifying all this must seem to her, to be left here with you and Mrs. Baker, and now me, surrounded by virtual strangers and unfamiliar things."

Though the scenario she painted was heartbreaking, John Lee was having a hard time focusing on anything but the warmth, the pressure of the body against his, the drugging scent of the perfume that wafted beneath his nose.

While he struggled to keep his mind fixed on the conversation at hand and not on the lustful thoughts that were forming, Merideth leaned back and tipped her face up to his. "She needs permanence, John Lee. She needs to know that her stay here isn't just temporary. She needs her own room, her own things. She needs to be surrounded with little-girl things, not a grown man's toys.'' She hugged his arm to her, holding it against her breast. ''You'll give her those things, won't you? Please tell me you will.''

John Lee had to give himself a firm mental shake to focus on the question and not on the enticing swell of breast pressed against his arm, on the blue eyes that looked up at him so pleadingly.

Of course he'd give Cassie those things, he told himself. He'd give her the whole damn house if he thought she needed it, or even wanted it. He adored her, and had since the moment he'd first laid eyes on her.

''All right,'' he replied gruffly. ''The room's hers.''

Merideth squealed and flung her arms around his neck. ''You are the best, John Lee Carter! The absolute best!''

Shocked at first by her exuberant display of gratitude, John Lee quickly recovered enough to wind his arms around her. When he did, she melted against him. Threading her fingers through his hair, she lifted her face to his.

A gentle smile played at her lips as she gazed up at him, her eyes all soft and warm, and John Lee forgot all about that promise he'd given her the day before about not making any more passes. With a low groan, he dipped his face to hers and slid his hands to the cheeks of her butt, drawing her intimately to him as he closed his mouth over hers. The taste was there, just as he remembered it, only maybe sweeter this time, hotter.

But just as he shifted to deepen the kiss, a rending sound came from the master bedroom. He snapped up his head in alarm, tearing his lips from Merideth's. A crash and the sound of glass shattering followed.

Jerking free of Merideth, he bolted for the door and found Bill on the ladder, holding one end of the wire, while Rudy stood on the other, holding the opposite end.

On the floor between them lay long, jagged shards of mirror.

John Lee's anger returned with a vengeance. Distracted first by the discovery of his gutted study, then by Merideth's warm and willing body, he'd forgotten all about Bill and Rudy and Merideth's instructions to them to remove the mirror from his bedroom wall. God only knew what else of his the woman planned to destroy.

"Good job, guys! I knew you could get it down."

He whirled to find Merideth standing behind him, smiling her praise at the two men.

He sucked in a breath, blinded by a rage that threatened to consume him. He should have known she had an ulterior motive when she'd cuddled up against him so willingly, especially after the fit she'd pitched the day before when he'd tried to kiss her. She'd probably thought that if she kept him occupied long enough, Rudy and Bill would have time to do her dirty work for her.

Well, she might have played him for a fool once, but not again.

He took a step toward her, narrowing his eyes as he bore down on her. "I may be willing to give up my study for Cassie, but *this* room," he said, stabbing a finger at the floor, "is mine, and nobody—and I do mean nobody—changes a thing. Understand?" Without waiting for an answer, he turned to glare at his men. "And if either one of you so much as lays a finger on that mirror on the ceiling, you'll be riding fence line for a month."

Merideth's mouth dropped open. "Surely you don't expect me to sleep beneath that hideous mirror?" she cried indignantly.

He slowly turned to look at her, his upper lip curling in a snarl. "Whether you choose to sleep under it or not is up to you. The mirror stays."

"But—"

John Lee lifted a finger in warning and Merideth snapped her mouth shut. Folding her arms across her breasts, she pursed her lips firmly together and glared at him.

He lowered his hand. "Now that we understand each other," he said, satisfied that he'd made his point. "I think it's time we all got back to work."

He turned to his men. "Bill, that tractor part you needed is waiting in the barn, and Rudy, I believe you've got some hay to haul." Without another word to Merideth, he strode for the door, both men following him.

"Understand each other, my foot," Merideth muttered under her breath as she watched the three men disappear into the hall. Avoiding the broken mirror, she marched to the phone and punched in a number.

Raking back her hair, she waited impatiently through three rings.

"Thomas," she purred at the sound of the male voice who answered. "It's Merideth, darling. Yes, it's been a long time," she replied, smiling. She wound the length of cord around her wrist, anxious to get to the point of her call. "Listen, darling, I find myself desperately in need of your creative touch. Would it be possible for you to drop by this afternoon? No," she said, shaking her head. "I'm not at the Double-Cross. I'm at John Lee Carter's. You know where his ranch is located, don't you? Good," she replied when he'd confirmed that he did. "About three? I'll see you then, darling."

Pleased with herself, Merideth dropped the phone back onto its base.

She tipped back her head and smiled at her reflection in the mirrored ceiling above the bed. "We'll just see who understands who, Mr. John Lee Carter," she said smugly.

Four

John Lee tiptoed down the hall, carrying his boots in his hand and weaving just a little. He wasn't drunk. Not really. Just relaxed. *Real* relaxed. He frowned, trying to remember how many beers he'd consumed, how many shots he'd tossed back, but quickly gave up. Didn't matter. The liquor had taken the edge off his anger and that had been his goal when he'd headed for the Waterin' Hole, the beer joint at the crossroads about five miles south of his ranch.

He supposed he should feel guilty for not returning to the house for dinner, or for at least stopping in to tell Merideth where he was going. But he didn't. Hell, it was her own damn fault if he'd avoided the house! She was the one who'd made him mad. She was the one who'd tied him up in knots by rubbing that hot little body of hers against his.

He'd tried working off his anger, his frustration, by

hauling hay with his wranglers till his arms ached and sweat was pouring down his back. But by quitting time, when his men had all headed for home, he discovered he still wasn't ready to face her again. Not after what she'd done.

Ripping the mirror off his wall! The nerve of that woman! No telling what changes she'd have made if he hadn't shown up when he had. She probably would've painted his bedroom pink and hung all kinds of frilly froufrou everywhere. He wouldn't put it past her.

And it was his room, by God! She might be using it for a while, but the room was still his and would be again long after she was gone. And if she didn't like his decor, that was too damn bad, because he did.

He'd put a lot of time and thought into redecorating the master bedroom after he'd retired from football and returned to his family's ranch to run it. The result was a pleasing blend of all sides of his personality and reflective of his life and his careers both as a professional athlete and as a cowboy.

He'd had a tough time finding a bed that suited him and had ended up having one made, and, along with it, the black satin down comforter, the upholstered cowhide headboard and the cushy pillows. An electrician had spent days hooking up the console beside his bed that controlled the lights and stereo. The man had charged a small fortune for his work, but the results were well worth the cost. With a twist of his finger, John Lee could fill his room with soft, romantic music or dim the lights. In his estimation, the mirrors on the ceiling and the wall had added the finishing touch.

Crooking an arm and stretching to relieve a sore muscle on his back, he stumbled to a stop outside his bedroom door. He'd just slip in and check on Cassie, he told himself, then he was going to soak in a tub for an hour.

Keeping his tread light so as not to wake Merideth, he stepped inside and headed straight for what once had been his den but was now Cassie's nursery. A nightlight glowed from an outlet beneath the window, allowing him to make out her small form in the crib.

His heart swelled almost painfully as he peered down at her. A miracle, he thought as he brushed a knuckle across her upturned cheek. So soft, so tiny, so perfect. He'd never dreamed that he'd feel this way about a baby, and as a confirmed bachelor who enjoyed the single life, had never planned to have any of his own. But this little gal had captured his heart the moment he'd laid eyes on her.

While he watched, mesmerized by her innocence, she drew in a shuddery breath, then released it on a sigh. Fearing he might wake her, he withdrew his hand and tucked the blanket to her chin. Unable to resist, he leaned over the side of the crib and pressed a kiss to her sweet cheek.

"'Night, Princess," he whispered.

Turning away, he tiptoed to the door and back into the master bedroom. The room was pitch-black, but that was the way John Lee had designed it. He didn't like sunlight waking him up in the morning before he was ready, so he'd had the drapes lined to keep even the smallest amount of light from filtering in.

Retracing his steps, he headed for the door and the hall beyond, anxious to get that bath. He hadn't taken three steps when his toe connected with something in the dark. "Damn," he muttered, grabbing for his foot and cradling his throbbing toe in his hand. He cut a glance toward the bed to see if the noise had awakened Merideth.

But he didn't see any movement. With the room as dark as it was, he could barely make out the outline of the bed, much less anything in it. Fearing Merideth might have run off in a huff, abandoning Cassie, after the words they'd had earlier, he set his boots aside and drew closer, but couldn't see anything but a tangle of bedcovers and a mountain of pillows. Frustrated, he propped one hand on the nightstand and the other on the mattress and leaned over until he was able to make out the top of her blond head buried between two pillows.

Satisfied that she was there and hadn't run out on him, he pushed himself away, using his hands for leverage….and inadvertently struck the line of switches on his nightstand's console. Light flooded the room while music swelled from the speakers.

He lunged at the console, frantically pushing at switches, trying to shut the lights and music off before they woke Merideth.

From the corner of his eye he caught a glimpse of arms flailing as Merideth fought her way free of the pillows. Her eyes wide, her mouth opening in a scream, she jack-knifed to a sitting position. Forgetting the switches, he dived across the bed and clamped a hand across her mouth.

"Don't scream," he begged in a whisper. "You'll wake the baby."

Her eyes riveted on his, she tore his fingers from her mouth. "What do you think you're doing?" she demanded angrily.

"I was checking on the baby and—"

"The baby doesn't sleep in here," she reminded him coldly. "*I* do! *She* sleeps in the nursery."

"Yeah, I know, and she's fine. I just checked on her."

She jerked the sheet across her lap. "Thanks for sharing," she snapped irritably.

With a huff, she collapsed against the padded headboard and raked her fingers through her hair. "What time is it, anyway?"

"A little after two."

She groaned and slid down the headboard, pulling a pillow over her head. "I'm going to hate you in the morning."

Maybe it was the beer, but John Lee couldn't help teasing her a little. "Why wait till morning?"

She lifted the pillow high enough to scowl up at him. "Fine. I hate you now."

"Aa-ww, Merideth," he said as he propped himself against the headboard beside her. "You don't want to hate me."

"Yes, I do," she argued, her voice muffled by the pillow. "You're mean and selfish and inconsiderate and you woke me up out of a sound sleep."

"Sure you didn't leave anything out?"

She lifted the pillow again. "As a matter of fact I did. You're also a pervert." With that, she slammed the pillow back over her face.

"A pervert?" he repeated in surprise. "And what makes me a pervert?"

"How many men do you know who would sneak into a woman's bedroom while she's sleeping, scare the daylights out of her, then climb into her bed?"

John Lee thought about that a minute, then shrugged. "None, but that certainly doesn't make me a pervert." He dug his shoulders deeper into the padded headboard, making himself more comfortable. "But since I'm here…" he added suggestively.

She dragged the pillow from her face to look up at him in disgust. "Honestly! Is sex all you think about?"

His position above her provided John Lee with an intriguing glimpse of the swell of her breasts. He grinned drunkenly at her. "Mostly." He scooted down on the bed until he was at eye level with her, then propped his elbow on her pillow and his cheek on his palm. "What do *you* think about?"

She drew her head back and narrowed an eye at him. "You're drunk, aren't you?"

His grinned broadened. "Nah. I just had a couple of beers with the boys down at the Waterin' Hole."

With a disapproving sniff, she pulled the sheet to her breasts. "I should've known that's where you went."

"Were you worried about me?"

"Hah! As if I cared enough to worry."

He continued to grin, knowing by her miffed look that she *had* worried. The thought pleased him. "You didn't answer my question," he reminded her. "What do you think about?"

She lifted her chin and smoothed the sheet across her chest. "What I think about is none of your business," she said airily.

"Aww, come on. You can tell me. I won't tell anybody."

"No," she repeated firmly.

"I'll bet you think about sex all the time."

"I most certainly do not!"

"Then what *do* you think about?"

"I don't know," she said, her patience wearing thin. "But it certainly isn't sex."

He had her rattled. He liked that. He also liked the shape of her nose. Not too short, not too long, and tipped up just a little at the end, kind of snooty-like. And her mouth. It was puckered in a pout at the moment, which emphasized the sharply defined bow on her upper lip. He had the strongest urge to place a kiss there.

"Want to make out?"

Her head snapped around, her brows bunching together above her nose. "I most certainly do not!"

He chuckled and scooted closer. "Sure you do. You just haven't given it any thought yet."

"There isn't anything to think about," she replied, and snapped her head back around to stare at the wall opposite her.

She was lying. John Lee could tell by the way her fingers were plucking at the edge of the sheet that she was thinking about it, all right. She just didn't want to admit it. But that was okay. He could be patient when he needed to be. And convincing.

"Personally, I like kissing," he said, dropping his voice to a whisper as if he was sharing a secret. "Feeling a woman's lips heat beneath mine, sipping at her own unique flavor and savoring it like it was a fine wine. No two women kiss alike. Did you know that?" he asked, though he didn't expect an answer from her—or want one, for that matter.

"Take you, for instance..." He lifted a hand to touch the tip of his finger against her lips. Though she flinched, she didn't move away, which only proved to him that he was right. She did want to kiss him. "This little bow on your lip," he went on to explain as he studied it carefully, "is more defined than most women's, which means that a man is more likely to feel it when he's kissing you.

"And when he moves his mouth across yours like this—" he smoothed his fingertip along her upper lip, demonstrating "—and his lips bump that little bow—" Even as he said it, his finger hit the bow, then slid over it. At the contact, he made a sound deep in his throat, humming his pleasure, then lifted his gaze to hers. "Sugar, let me tell you, that is one of the most erotic sensations a man can experience, short of burying himself inside a woman."

Transfixed, Merideth could only stare at him. From the moment he'd started talking, his voice low and seductive, he'd captured her, luring her in with his words and with his touch until she was nothing but a bundle of raw nerves. How he'd done it, she didn't know, and really didn't care. All she knew was that she wanted, needed more than his finger on her lips.

Her mouth suddenly dry, she wet her lips with her tongue. "John Lee," she whispered, and heard the quiver in her voice.

"Yeah, sugar?"

"I've thought about it, and I've decided that I would like to make out with you, after all."

His smile broadened. "Is that a fact?" He scooted closer. "Well, sugar, I'd be more than happy to accommodate you."

And he did. For the next few minutes, he devoted himself to showing Merideth the pleasures to be found in two mouths mating. Butterfly kisses across the lips that left her quivering. Deep thrusts of his tongue that echoed in her womb and left her gasping. Tender nibbles at her lips that made her hungry for more.

They probably could have kissed all night, but a soft whimper from the nursery made them separate. Their eyes met, hers glazed with passion, his with regret at the interruption.

"Cassie," she whispered, her eyes riveted on his. "I'll check on her." Before he could stop her, she'd scooted from the bed and hurried across the room.

With a lusty sigh, John Lee rolled to his back and watched her disappear beyond the nursery door, enjoying the length of bare leg the night light revealed. He heard her rustling around in the other room, the sound of her voice gently soothing. As he stared at the dark opening, waiting for her to reappear, his eyelids grew heavy. From weariness or from the amount of liquor he'd consumed he wasn't sure, but he found it harder and harder to keep them open.

I'll just rest them a minute, he told himself as he laced his fingers across his chest and closed his eyes. Just for a minute, then—

Before he finished the thought, he was snoring.

John Lee wanted to open his eyes, but he was afraid to. He feared if he did, the horrific pounding in his head would shoot his eyeballs straight out of their sockets and across the room. The pressure behind them was that intense.

Tequila, he remembered, groaning. What had possessed him to do tequila shots when he knew damn good and well the stuff gave him a hangover to beat all hangovers?

He cracked open his lips to wet them with his tongue. Water. He needed water. And aspirin. A handful, at least. Nothing less would do, he was sure.

"John Lee?"

His name was like an explosion at his ear and he grabbed for his head to keep it from splitting wide open.

"What's wrong, darling? Do you have a headache?"

Merideth? Merideth, he remembered with a groan. And if he wasn't mistaken, a very smug-sounding Merideth, who was more than aware of his pain. If he hadn't needed his hands to keep his head on, he'd have been tempted to clamp them over her mouth to keep her quiet.

"Please," he whispered, his voice rusty. "Have mercy."

Her laugh was low and throaty and sent a new fissure cracking through his skull.

"The devil will always have his due," she quoted smugly.

He moaned at her lack of sympathy.

Holding his hands in readiness, just in case his eyeballs did in fact pop out and he needed to catch them, he opened his eyes a sliver.

Merideth lay opposite him, watching him. She smiled and raised a hand to brush his hair from his forehead. "Are you going to live?"

Her touch was butterfly-soft and oddly soothing. "Maybe. The jury's still out."

She chuckled and drew her palm to his face, feathering the ball of her thumb beneath his eye while her palm skimmed his cheek. "You bombed on me last night."

Well, that was certainly one way to put it, he thought ruefully. Beat the hell out of "passed out," which was exactly what he'd done when she'd gone to check on the baby.

"I did, didn't I?" he said with regret.

"Yes, you did." She centered the ball of her thumb at his temple and gently massaged. "A shame, too, because I was really enjoying making out with you." She wiggled closer. "You were really making me hot," she whispered against his ear. "If you hadn't gone to sleep…"

Instead of finishing the statement, she let it hang, allowing John Lee's imagination to fill in the gap. He closed his eyes, moaning his frustration as he imagined Merideth all hot and needy and crawling back into bed with him only to find him asleep. "You're doing this on purpose, aren't you?" he asked miserably.

"Doing what?"

"You're punishing me for passing out on you, aren't you?"

"Who, me?"

Her reply was a little too innocent to be believable and had John Lee cracking open an eye and frowning at her.

She tossed back her head and laughed at his sour look.

He winced and flattened a hand over his ear. "Please," he begged. "I'm dying here."

Covering his hand with hers, she pressed her lips to his forehead. "Poor baby," she murmured sympathetically, though he could still hear the amusement in her voice. "What can I do to help?"

"Aspirin. In the drawer by the sink in the bathroom. And water," he added desperately as she slipped from the bed.

He rolled to his back, holding his head on with his hands while he waited. She returned seconds later and crawled onto the bed to kneel beside him.

"Thank you," he murmured gratefully as he pushed himself up on his elbow. But when he reached for the aspirins she offered, it put him almost nose to nipple with her breasts. As his gaze locked on that dark circle of lusciousness peeking from behind the thin silk, the pounding in his head shifted lower. Much lower. He quickly tossed back the aspirins, then washed them down with the water. Pushing the glass in the general direction of the bedside table, he wrapped his arm around her waist and pulled her down on top of him.

"John Lee!" she gasped as he closed his mouth over a lace-covered breast.

"Hmmm?" he murmured, flicking his tongue against a knotted bud.

She arched, dropping back her head. "Oh, my," she said on a lusty sigh.

"Well, I never!"

John Lee bolted upright at the sound of his housekeeper's voice, flipping Merideth off him and to his side. "Mrs. Baker!" he croaked. "What are you doing here?"

Merideth groaned and buried her face in the mattress, wishing she could melt into it.

"I came to tell you your breakfast is ready, same as I do every morning of the world. And here you are shacked up with that woman!"

Merideth heard the condemnation in Mrs. Baker's voice and turned her head to frown at her over her shoulder. Mrs. Baker returned the look, her lips pinched tight in disapproval.

With a resigned sigh, Merideth rolled over and scooted to a sitting position beside John Lee, pulling the sheet to her chin.

"I'm sorry, Mrs. Baker," he murmured. "I didn't realize the time. I'll be right there."

"Humph! If you can tear yourself away from that tramp!"

Merideth sat up, her spine arrow straight. "Tramp!" she repeated as she watched the woman turn and march away. She turned to look at John Lee, her eyes wide in dismay. "Did you hear her? She called me a tramp!"

John Lee's headache returned with a vengeance. "I'm sure she didn't mean anything by it," he said, rubbing at his temple. "She's just upset."

"*She's* upset!" Merideth flounced back against the headboard, folding her arms beneath her breasts. "*I'm* the one who should be upset."

Hoping to console her, at the very least quiet her, he wrapped an arm around her shoulders and drew her to his side. "Now, Merideth," he began patiently.

She gave his leg a sound kick, refusing to be coddled. "Don't you 'now, Merideth' me. It wasn't you who got called a name."

John Lee pressed his nose in the crook of her neck and nuzzled. "I did last night. I distinctly remember you calling me a pervert."

She hunched her shoulder, trying not to let his mouth distract her from her anger. "Yes, but you deserved it."

He chuckled and reached around her, wrapping an arm at her waist and turning her on her side. Angling his mouth over hers, he teased her lower lip with his teeth. "If enjoying kissing a beautiful woman like you is a perversion, then, yeah, I guess I'm a pervert."

She batted at him, trying not to smile. "You are insatiable."

"Yeah, I guess I am." He snuggled closer. "Want to make out?"

Merideth let go of her anger and with it a little sigh. "Are you going to bomb out on me again?"

"Not if I can help it."

Dressed in silk lounging pajamas, Merideth sat on the floor of the nursery, stacking blocks of varying colors and sizes into a semblance of a house. Cassie sat opposite her, eyes wide, watching.

"What do you think? Do we need a window here?" Merideth asked as she put another block in place.

Cassie chortled and clapped her chubby hands.

"I must say, you have an excellent eye for detail," she complimented the baby as she rearranged blocks so that a space appeared. After making another adjustment or two, she leaned back to admire her work. "There," she said, nodding her approval of the design. "A beautiful castle for my little princess."

Cassie dived forward, and with a sweep of her little hands, sent the blocks tumbling. Lying flat on her stomach among the scattered blocks, she grinned up at Merideth, obviously proud of her accomplishment.

Laughing, Merideth scooped her up and swung her high in the air. "That makes three of my houses you've destroyed, you little battering ram. I think it's time for a break." She rose, shifting Cassie to her hip, and crossed to the intercom. Pressing a button, she spoke into the speaker. "Mrs. Baker?"

"Yeah?" came the housekeeper's sour response.

"You can bring the tray to the nursery. We're ready for our snack now." Without waiting for an answer, she switched the intercom off. "Disagreeable old woman," she muttered.

They'd been butting heads all morning, with the woman snarling and complaining every time Merideth made the simplest request.

It had all started with the fried eggs the housekeeper had shoved in front of Merideth at breakfast. Not that Merideth was opposed to fried eggs, she just hadn't been in the mood for them that morning and had asked instead for scrambled ones with a touch of dill. By the way Mrs. Baker's eyes had bugged, a person would have thought Merideth had asked her to *lay* an egg, not scramble one. She'd grumbled and complained so much that by the time she plopped the plate of scrambled eggs on the table, Merideth had lost her appetite for them. And that had *really* set the old biddy on her ear!

And then there was the little incident over the blouse Merideth planned to wear to dinner that night. She'd merely asked Mrs. Baker to press it, which the house-keeper had finally done, but not without ranting and raving and carrying on for hours about how much extra work Merideth was heaping on her shoulders.

It was John Lee's fault, Merideth concluded. He allowed the woman entirely too much freedom.

She gave Cassie a quick squeeze. "Don't ever let your employees get the upper hand," she lectured prudently. "If you do, they become lazy and disrespectful."

In answer, Cassie snuggled against Merideth's breast, rubbing at her eyes. "Are you sleepy?" Merideth asked, then pressed her fingers to her own mouth, stifling a yawn. "Me, too," she murmured. "Your Uncle John Lee kept me up most of the night."

"Where do you want it?"

Merideth turned at the sound of the housekeeper's surly voice to find her standing in the door, tray in hand. "I'm sorry, Mrs. Baker, but we've decided to forego the snack in lieu of a nap, so it seems we won't need the tray after all." Ignoring the woman's frown, she added, "But we will need Cassie's bottle. Would you bring it to us, please?"

With a huff, the woman spun and stomped away.

"A perfect example of what I was talking about," Merideth noted, frowning, then she smiled, giving Cassie another little squeeze. "But don't worry. We'll have her whipped into shape in no time."

Confident that she would, Merideth crossed to the rocker and settled herself comfortably. Pushing a bare foot against the plush carpet, she set the rocker in motion and waited, imagining the room with the all the new furniture she'd ordered. In no time she'd have this room looking like a real nursery, she told herself.

Mrs. Baker returned and shoved the bottle under Merideth's nose.

Arching a brow, Merideth murmured a thank-you, then shifted Cassie to the crook of her arm and offered her the bottle. Closing her chubby hands around it, the baby pulled it to her mouth and began to suck greedily.

"Make sure you burp her, 'fore you put her down for her nap," Mrs. Baker warned. "Otherwise she'll get gas."

That the woman would have the nerve to tell her what to do, didn't set well with Merideth. "You needn't worry," she replied arrogantly. "I know how to care for a baby."

The woman snorted her disagreement, which angered Merideth all the more. Deciding that now was as good as any to put her in her place, Merideth shook back her hair and settled against the rocker. "I noticed that there were only a few towels remaining in the linen closet in the master bath. You might want to replenish the supply."

"There'd be more towels if you didn't use four of 'em every time you bathed yourself."

Merideth refused to qualify the woman's subordination with a response. "And you might as well as change the linens on the bed while you're at it," she said. "I'll want to rest after I put Cassie down for her nap."

"Rest!" the woman exclaimed. "What do you need to rest for? You haven't broken a sweat all morning!"

Merideth sucked in a shocked breath. "I beg your pardon?"

"*I'm* the one who needs a rest," Mrs. Baker complained, stabbing a thumb at her chest. "Cooking and cleaning and running back and forth every time you squawk a command in that dang intercom."

"Squawk?" Merideth repeated in horror. "I'll have you know I have a beautifully modulated voice. All my speech instructors have said so."

"Must be tone deaf, the lot of 'em, or their ears were plugged with wax, 'cause you squawk and on occasion even screech."

Furious, Merideth tightened her arms around Cassie and rose. "How dare you insult me that way! John Lee will hear about this."

"'John Lee will hear about this,'" the housekeeper mocked. "Well, tell him whatever you dang please, 'cause I quit!" She whirled, stripping off her apron and flung it on the floor as she stormed from the room.

Trembling with rage, Merideth yelled after her, "You can't quit because I'm firing you."

At the commotion, Cassie popped the nipple from her mouth, and started howling. Merideth took the bottle from her and shifted her to her shoulder. Pacing, she patted furiously at her back. "The witch," she muttered angrily. "Who does she think she is, talking to me like that? Well, good riddance, that's what I say! John Lee will thank me for getting rid of the old shrew."

Hungrier than a bear after a long winter nap, John Lee stepped into the kitchen, sniffing the air. His wranglers trooped in behind him.

Puzzled when no mouthwatering scents greeted him, John Lee glanced around, then frowned when he saw that the stove was bare and the table wasn't even set for lunch. "Mrs. Baker?" he called. When he didn't hear a response, he tossed his hat to the counter. "You boys get washed up and I'll see if I can find her."

He checked the laundry room, the den, his house-keeper's usual haunts, then headed for the master bedroom. Inside, he found Merideth curled up on the bed, asleep. A feeling of dread swept over him when he saw the crumpled apron lying on the floor. Crossing to the bed, he reached down and gave Merideth's shoulder a hard shake. "Merideth, wake up."

She groaned and rolled to her back, scraping her hair from her face. "What time is it?" she asked sleepily.

"Noon. Where is Mrs. Baker? I can't find her anywhere."

Merideth dropped her hands, then rolled to her side, pulling the pillow back beneath her head. "I fired her," she murmured.

"Fired her!" John Lee roared. He grabbed her by the arm and hauled her to a sitting position. "What do you mean, you fired her?"

Irritated by his rough treatment, Merideth jerked free of his arm. "Exactly that. I fired her." She pursed her lips, remembering. "The woman is a shrew. She said that I squawk when I speak."

"So you fired her?"

Merideth lifted her chin. "I certainly did. She should've been fired long ago. You should thank me for saving you the trouble."

"Thank you!" he yelled. "You spoiled little brat! Do you realize what you've done?"

Merideth sucked in a furious breath. *A spoiled little brat?* No one ever spoke to her in that tone of voice! No one! And if they'd dared, she wouldn't have hesitated to verbally rip them to shreds. But there was something in John Lee's eyes, in the tautness of his jaw, that stripped her of her retort.

He threw out an arm, a rigid finger pointing toward the other end of the house. "There are ten hungry men standing in the kitchen right now, waiting for their lunch, a lunch that Mrs. Baker usually cooks, serves, and cleans up after.''

Merideth winced. ''She did all that?''

With an impatient growl, he grabbed her arm and dragged from the bed. ''Yes, she did that, and more!''

He snatched the apron from the floor and slung it around Merideth's waist, tying it behind her back, then gave her a shove toward the door.

Tripping over her feet, Merideth cast a frantic glance over her shoulder. ''Surely you don't intend for me—''

''Yes, I certainly do,'' he said through clenched teeth. ''You fired the woman who usually cooks for them, so you can damn well see that they don't go hungry.''

Merideth swallowed hard. ''But, John Lee—''

''No buts,'' he warned dangerously. ''I'm going to get Cassie up, and when I get to the kitchen, you better be there and there better be food on the table.''

The tone of his voice told Merideth that arguing would do her no good.

But I can't cook, she cried silently as she turned for the door. I don't know how! I've never *needed* to know how! I've always had servants to do the cooking for me.

At the kitchen door, she stopped and gave herself a firm shake. You can do this, she told herself, trying not to think of the ten hungry men who awaited her on the other side of the door. You are ten times more intelligent than that silly old Mrs. Baker, and if she can prepare a meal for these men, then you can, too. She gave the collar of her lounging pajamas a firm snap, then smoothed the wrinkles from her apron, stalling for time.

But when she pushed through the door and ten sets of eyes turned to look at her expectantly, she froze. The men looked hungry and mean and a vision rose of them dragging her outside, staking her on the ground and letting the ants have her, once they realized she'd fired their cook. It was all she could do to keep from turning tail and running back to the master bedroom and hiding under the bed. But she couldn't. John Lee would just drag her back out, if she did.

She'd just have to bluff her way through this, she told herself. Forcing a smile, she swept into the room. "Hi, guys," she greeted them cheerfully. "Seems there's a little problem. Mrs. Baker—" At the mention of Mrs Baker's name, to a man, their eyes narrowed suspiciously and Merideth decided a small lie might prove beneficial to her continued good health. "Well, she had to leave unexpectedly," she explained vaguely. "But don't worry about a thing. I'll have your lunch on the table in no time flat."

Praying that Mrs. Baker had already prepared the meal before she left, she peeked inside the oven. Her heart sank when she found it empty and cold. With a nervous glance over her shoulder, she found the men watching her. Offering them a trembling smile, she closed the oven door and hurried on to the refrigerator. She tugged open the door and leaned to peer inside. Milk. Bread. A gallon of orange juice. A tray of eggs. Several jars of baby food. Leftover meat loaf. She groaned inwardly and pressed her forehead against the edge of the refrigerator door, staring at the meager offerings. There wasn't anything that looked like it would come close to feeding ten men, and even if there was, she wasn't sure she'd know what to do with it.

The swinging door creaked open behind her and she glanced over her shoulder to see John Lee entering with Cassie propped on his hip. Tears stung her eyes. She couldn't bluff her way through this, she told herself miserably. She didn't know how to cook. At least not for a bunch of starving men. "John Lee..."

He must have seen the desperation in her eyes, because he plopped Cassie into her high chair and belted her in, then headed for the refrigerator. "Sandwiches," he said. "Ham sandwiches," he clarified, shooting her a dark look as he tugged open the meat keeper and pulled out a covered plate of sliced ham. "Isn't that what you said we were having for lunch?"

"Yes," Merideth whispered gratefully, then with more feeling, "Yes! Ham sandwiches." She grabbed item after item from the refrigerator, filling her arms with mustard and mayonnaise, pickles and condiments.

She knew how to make sandwiches, she thought with relief. In fact, she considered herself rather a connoisseur, having assisted her own housekeeper in making a platter of them for a cocktail party she'd hosted in the not-so-distant past. Of course, her sandwiches had been filled with thinly sliced cucumbers and smoked salmon, not thick slices of ham, but the process was the same to her way of thinking.

While the men sat around the table talking, Merideth made two more trips to the refrigerator, then quickly laid out slices of bread and smeared them all with a light coating of mustard and mayonnaise. Taking the plate of meat John Lee had set out for her, she carefully arranged thick slices of ham on each, then topped them off with cheese and another slice of bread.

With a nervous glance at the men huddled around the table behind her, she picked up the knife again and began painstakingly slicing the crust from the bread. After dumping the scraps into the disposal, she cut the sandwiches into tiny squares and triangles and arranged them on a platter. Eyeing the sandwiches critically, she opened a jar of olives, lanced one with a toothpick, then stuck it in the center of one of the triangles.

Perfect, she thought, then repeated the process on each sandwich, varying the color scheme with first black and then pimento-stuffed green olives. Next, she fanned pickles around the edges of the platter.

"Aren't those sandwiches ready yet?" John Lee complained loudly.

"Just about," she called cheerfully, delighted with her accomplishment. Grabbing a scraper from the drawer, she shaved long curls of carrot and scattered them among the sandwiches. Lifting the platter, she smiled, pleased with both her skill and the presentation.

"Here you are, boys," she said proudly and set the platter in the center of the table. Clasping her hands beneath her chin, she stepped back and waited for their praise.

But nobody said a word, they all just sat there and stared at the huge platter of sandwiches.

Except for John Lee.

He shoved back from his chair and threw his napkin to the table in disgust. "For God's sake, Merideth," he growled. "This isn't some damn tea party. Can't you do anything right?"

Five

Her arms full, Merideth juggled the baby and the bulging diaper bag to one side but couldn't quite stretch a hand far enough to reach the doorknob. Frustrated, she pressed her nose against the glass panel on the Double-Cross's kitchen door and saw Mandy standing in front of the stove, steam billowing around her head.

With her own culinary failure so fresh on her mind, finding her sister cooking infuriated Merideth even more. She gave the door a hard bump with her knee. "Mandy! Open the door!"

Mandy spun, a smile curving her lips when she saw Merideth. She quickly switched off the flame beneath the large stew pot and hurried across the room. But when she opened the door and saw that Merideth was dressed in a pair of silk lounging pajamas, her mouth sagged open.

"Merideth!" she cried. With a frantic glance around to see if anyone had witnessed her sister's arrival, she tugged Merideth inside the house and quickly closed the door behind her. "What are you doing running around the countryside half-dressed?" she scolded as she took Cassie from her arms. "And in your bare feet, no less!"

Ignoring Mandy's criticism, Merideth flung the diaper bag in the direction of the table and stormed across the room. "I hate him!" she raged, running her hands through her hair.

The dramatics were pure Merideth and wasted on Mandy. She'd witnessed better displays of temper than this from her sister, but she was curious as to who had set this one off. She shifted Cassie to her hip. "Who do you hate?"

Merideth spun, her body trembling with rage. "John Lee Carter! That's who! He is mean and hateful and I hope he chokes on his stupid ham sandwiches!"

Mandy sputtered a laugh, but Cassie, who, up until this point, had watched Merideth's hysterics in round-eyed silence, suddenly burst into tears.

Immediately Merideth wilted, rushing to take Cassie from Mandy. She pursed her mouth sympathetically as she drew her into her arms. "There, there, darling," she soothed, swaying gently. "Merideth didn't mean to frighten you."

Merideth's mood swing from enraged woman to nurturing nanny was so quick it made Mandy dizzy just to watch. Sighing, she picked up the diaper bag and set it on the table, digging through its jumbled contents until she found a bottle of juice. She handed it to Merideth.

"Thank you," Merideth murmured gratefully, and sank down on a kitchen chair. Shifting Cassie, to cradle her in her arms, she teased her mouth with the nipple. The crying instantly stopped as Cassie latched on to the bottle and began to suck.

The naturalness and the affection with which Merideth handled the baby didn't escape Mandy's notice, though she decided it wise under the circumstances not to comment on it. Instead she sank down on a chair opposite her. "Maybe you better tell me what has you so upset."

At the reminder, Merideth lifted her gaze, tears filling her eyes. "Oh, Mandy," she sobbed miserably. "I can't cook."

At the unexpected confession, Mandy tossed back her head and laughed. "Well, of course you can't. You've never had to."

"It isn't funny," Merideth wailed. "I'm in big trouble."

"Trouble?" Mandy repeated, sobering. "How does not being able to cook put you in trouble?"

Merideth snatched a napkin from the holder on the table and dabbed at her cheeks. "I fired John Lee's housekeeper."

"You didn't!"

Merideth firmed her lips, jutting her chin defensively. "I most certainly did. The woman was insolent and lazy."

"And John Lee expects *you* to take over her responsibilities?"

Fresh tears welled up and Merideth pressed the napkin against her lips. "Yes."

Mandy tossed up her hands. "But you don't know how to cook!"

"I know," Merideth wailed. "Oh, Mandy, it was horrible! After Mrs. Baker left, I lay down, thinking I'd take a little nap while Cassie slept, then John Lee came home with all his wranglers for lunch. When I told him that Mrs. Baker was gone and that I had fired her, he dragged me out of bed and told me that since her leaving was all my fault, I had to make lunch for all those men.''

''And did you?''

Merideth pressed a knuckle beneath her nose and nodded, sniffing back the tears. ''At first I didn't know what to do, but then John Lee came in and suggested I make ham sandwiches. I was relieved, because I *know* how to make sandwiches. In fact, I have quite a flair for them. My housekeeper, Lilah, told me so.

''I worked really fast, too, knowing the men must be hungry. I sliced all the edges off the bread, careful not to leave so much as a trace of the brown outer crust, just like Lilah taught me, then I cut the sandwiches into clever little squares and triangles. I even scattered carrot curls around the platter for added color, which I thought was truly inspired, considering I had so little to work with. But when I put the sandwiches on the table, John Lee, he—he—'' She pressed the napkin to her lips as a new wave of sobs rose, choking her.

Mandy leaned forward expectantly. ''He what?''

''H-he said, 'For God's sake, M-Merideth. This isn't s-some damn tea party. C-can't you do anything right?''' She dropped an elbow to the table and pressed her hand over her mouth, sobbing uncontrollably. ''Oh, Mandy, it was terrible!'' she cried. ''I felt like such a fool!''

Though Mandy could imagine—and even understand—John Lee's consternation when presented with such a skimpy and fussy lunch when what he and his men were accustomed to receiving was a hot noonday meal, her heart went out to Merideth who had tried so hard to please. She stretched a hand across the table to squeeze her sister's arm in sympathy. ''Oh, sweetheart, there are worse things in life than not being able to cook.''

Merideth jerked free of her, refusing to be comforted. "Easy for you to say. You know how to cook!" Snatching a fresh napkin from the holder, she dabbed furiously at her eyes, then blotted the drop of juice that had leaked from the corner of Cassie's mouth. "I can't even make sandwiches to please him and his stupid wranglers," she moaned in despair, taking the bottle from the now sleeping Cassie. "How on earth am I supposed to cook a real meal for them?"

That Merideth would even consider attempting to cook for the men, especially after John Lee had insulted her first attempt, surprised Mandy. It would have been much more in character for her to tell them all to go straight to hell.

Could Merideth be mellowing? Mandy wondered. Or did this change have something to do with John Lee? Whatever the reason, as long as Merideth was willing to try her hand at domesticity, Mandy would do everything in her power to help her. "I'll teach you."

Merideth snapped up her head at the offer. "Do you think you could?" she asked, her uncertainty obvious.

Mandy rose, smiling confidently. "Honey, by the time I get through with you, John Lee'll think Martha Stewart has moved in."

Merideth shoved the last container of food into the freezer and slammed the door, then leaned back against it. She was tired. No, she was exhausted. But by golly she had some food in the freezer, enough to keep John Lee and those wranglers of his satisfied for a week.

Patting her pocket to make sure Mandy's warming instructions were still there, she headed for the bedroom. She'd already put Cassie to bed for the night, and she intended to follow suit.

As she passed through the bedroom doorway, she started stripping, dropping clothes on the floor as she made her way to the bed. Too tired to worry with a nightgown, she flung back the covers and crawled between the cool satin sheets. She leaned over to push the tab on the bedside table, turning off the lights, and noticed the time. Nine-thirty. She would've laughed if she hadn't been so tired. Merideth McCloud in bed before midnight. This had to be a first.

With a sigh, she collapsed against the pillows and closed her eyes. She'd had no idea that cooking could be so exhausting. Her feet ached, her back ached. Even her hands ached from all the kneading. For a moment—no longer than a second, really—she actually felt a twinge of empathy for Mrs. Baker and the work required of her to cook for all those men.

She quickly shrugged it off and rolled to her side, curling into a ball and tucking her hands beneath her cheek. No, she wouldn't feel sorry for the woman.

After all, she had called Merideth a tramp.

When John Lee stepped into the kitchen, he was greeted with darkness and an eerie silence, both of which worried him. He'd checked the garage on his way in and verified that his Porsche was once again parked in its space, a sure sign that Merideth had returned from the Double-Cross which was where he was certain she'd headed when she'd taken off in such a huff earlier that day.

Judging by the quiet, though, and the lack of light, he was beginning to wonder if maybe it was only his Porsche that had returned, that Merideth had stayed at the Double-Cross and sent someone else to deliver his car.

It was a possibility, considering the snit she'd been in when she'd left.

He frowned, remembering the flash of her hurt in her eyes when he'd yelled at her, then the steely-eyed fury that had followed. Without a word to him, she'd snatched Cassie from the high chair, slammed an arm around a diaper bag propped on the kitchen counter and stormed out the back door.

He hadn't tried to stop her. Hadn't wanted to. His own anger wouldn't let him. Hell! he thought defensively. She'd fired his housekeeper—the woman he depended on to feed his men and to keep his house running smoothly. He had a right to be mad at her.

But as hard as he tried to rekindle his anger, he couldn't. It was gone. He'd burned it off with a hammer, a pound of fencing staples and a tightly coiled roll of barbed wire. His reward at the end of the day was a quarter mile of newly stretched barbed wire, a considerable drop in his blood pressure…and the unwanted task of trying to undo the damage that Merideth had done.

He'd gone to Mrs. Baker's house, hat in hand, to throw himself on her mercy. He'd apologized profusely for whatever sins Merideth had committed and had begged her to return. But the woman wouldn't budge. In fact, the way she'd carried on, he wondered at her sanity. She kept mumbling something about that tramp Charise, and John Lee had had a time trying to keep her focused on his apology. In the end, she'd told him that as long as "that woman," as she liked to refer to Merideth, was in his house, she wasn't setting a foot inside. Either Merideth went, or no housekeeper. That was the choice left to him.

With a sigh, John Lee tossed his hat to the counter and wearily raked his fingers through his hair. So what was he supposed to do now? He couldn't ask Merideth to leave. Didn't want to. His purpose in inviting her into his home was to help her get over the loss of her baby and to help him with Cassie. And it was working. From the moment she'd announced that she was moving in, he'd seen a change in Merideth. She was acting more like her old self—bossy, cantankerous, full of spit and vinegar...and downright sexy.

He rubbed a hand across his mouth, remembering the kissing session in bed the night before and again that morning. Yeah, she was sexy all right, and about as hard to resist as a cold beer on a hot day. If only she could cook...

He wagged his head, remembering that ridiculous platter of sandwiches she'd made for his men, the look of hurt in her eyes when he'd yelled at her. He should have known Merideth didn't know her way around a kitchen. Demanding that she cook for his men was a mistake that he'd regretted for the rest of the day.

Truth of the matter was, the whole dang situation could have been avoided if he'd put a stop to the bickering between the two women before it got so out of hand. It wasn't as if he hadn't known that Mrs. Baker hated Merideth, though he hadn't a clue why. Or that Merideth disliked her, for that matter. Neither had tried to hide their feelings from him. They were like two old billy goats going head-to-head.

Granted, Merideth hadn't helped matters any by ordering Mrs. Baker around. But then, why had he expected anything less from Merideth? She was accustomed to getting her own way, to being the center of attention, of having everyone wait on her hand and foot. Her sisters spoiled her, her fans adored her, her peers sucked up to her, hoping to snag a part of the spotlight always directed her way. It was only natural that Merideth would rebel against someone who refused to pay her what she considered her due.

And it wasn't as if Merideth hadn't warned him. She'd told him up front that her sole purpose in moving in with him was to care for Cassie, that she didn't cook, clean or do laundry, including her own.

He sighed again, knowing he was responsible for the mess he was currently mired in. He'd already offered Mrs. Baker an apology, though it hadn't done him any good. Now he owed Merideth one. A big one. And putting it off wasn't going to make it any easier to offer. Knowing this, he headed for the swinging door, praying that he'd find her in his room. The thought of driving all the way to the Double-Cross and having to apologize to Merideth in front of her sisters didn't set well with him at all. He'd done enough groveling for one day.

When he reached the master bedroom and saw that the lights were off, he started to turn away, thinking she had stayed at the Double-Cross, but a whisper of satin from the direction of the bed made him turn back. Squinting against the darkness, he tiptoed toward the bed and peered down. Sure enough, a cap of blond hair peeked out from between two pillows.

With a sigh of relief, he settled a hip on the edge of the mattress and leaned over. "Merideth?" he whispered. When she didn't respond, he pulled one of the pillows away from her head. "Merideth," he repeated more insistently.

"Hmmm?"

"Are you asleep?"

"Yes," she groaned. "Go away."

Biting back a grin, he plucked the other pillow from

beside her head and tossed it aside. "Can't. I've got something to say."

She grabbed the sheet and pulled it over her head. "I don't want to hear it."

"Sure you do." Wanting to see her face so that he could determine her mood and know how much bending and scraping he was going to have to do, he stretched a hand to the bedside table. He pushed a finger against a tab until the soft glow from the recessed lights chased away some of the darkness.

At the intrusion, Merideth fisted the sheet tighter over her face. "Would you *please* go away?"

Though there was a please in the request, her tone was anything but pleasant.

"Not until I say what I've come to say." Angling a knee onto the mattress, John Lee folded his hands over his thigh and turned to look at her shrouded form, determined to get this over with. "I'm sorry, Merideth."

He waited a beat, hoping for a response, but the only sign that she'd heard his apology was a subtle relaxing of her fingers on the sheet. Then slowly the sheet inched down, revealing first a tangle of blond hair, a smooth forehead, neatly arched brows, then eyes, a startled blue. It stopped at the bridge of her nose. "What did you say?"

"I said, I'm sorry."

The sheet dropped another few inches, exposing the tip of her turned-up nose and that luscious mouth of hers, but stopped at her chin. "For what?"

He should have known she wouldn't just accept his apology outright, that she'd make him crawl first. He gritted his teeth and forced himself to say it all. "I had no call to yell at you today, and I apologize if I hurt your feelings. Will you forgive me?"

She drew her arms from beneath the sheet and flattened

them over it, stretching the satin across her breasts. She smiled smugly. "I'm glad that you've seen the error of your ways, because you're right, your actions *were* totally unjustified." She pursed her lips and tapped a manicured nail against them as she studied him thoughtfully. "But I'm not sure I'm willing to forgive you. After all, you did hurt my feelings."

John Lee tossed up his hands in frustration. "For God's sake! I said I'm sorry! What else can I say?"

She drew back her chin, arching a brow. "What else can you say?" she asked pointedly. "Why, nothing. But there is a lot you can *do.*"

"Oh, for crying out loud, Merideth," he grumbled.

"You do want my forgiveness, don't you?"

"Well, yeah, but—"

She sat up and leaned to press a finger to his lips, holding the sheet against her breasts. "No buts, John Lee," she reminded him. "Isn't that what you always tell me?" She smiled, obviously enjoying the fact that she had him over a barrel. Scooching backwards, she propped herself against the headboard, looking a little too pleased with herself.

"There is the problem with Cassie's nursery," she began.

A sick feeling settled in John Lee's stomach. He wasn't at all sure what she was about to demand of him, because he'd already given up his den to Cassie, but he had a feeling that Merideth's dissatisfaction with his bedroom's decor entered into the picture somewhere, probably at the top of her list.

"As I recall," she reminded him, "you refused to allow your men to help me paint it—"

Pressing a hand over his heart, John Lee fell over onto his side, weak with relief.

He landed on her legs, and Merideth gave his shoulder an impatient kick with her foot. "Get off of me!"

Closing his hand around her ankle to keep her from kicking him again, he looked up at her. "For a minute there, I was afraid you were going to make me take down the mirror from the ceiling."

She immediately quit struggling, smiling slyly. "Oh, I've already taken care of that tacky old mirror."

He flipped his eyes wide. "You what!" Sure that she had somehow managed to remove the mirror without his knowing it, John Lee rolled to his back and looked up. Instead of his mirror, yards and yards of a shimmering gold fabric were draped over the ceiling above him and came together in a huge rosette over the center of the bed.

Merideth sat up again, holding the sheet in place beneath her arms, and leaned over to pat his cheek. "Don't worry," she assured him. "Your disgusting mirror is still there. I just covered it up."

John Lee closed his eyes, his shoulders sagging in relief. "Thank goodness," he murmured. When he opened his eyes, Merideth was still leaning over him. That she was pleased with the success of her subterfuge was obvious. He frowned at her. "You're a brat, you know it?"

She lifted a shoulder, her smile broadening. "That's what they tell me."

That little shrug drew John Lee's gaze to her shoulder and to the amount of bare skin exposed above the sheet. He wondered what, if anything, she was wearing beneath it. He traced a finger along her collarbone. "What do you have on underneath that sheet?"

She shivered at the touch of his hand against her skin. "Nothing."

He shifted his gaze to hers, the tip of his finger stilling

at the base of her throat. Beneath it he felt the quickening of her pulse. "Nothing?" he repeated.

A slow smile curved her lips. "Not a stitch."

It wasn't an invitation really, but John Lee figured it was close enough. After all, it wasn't every day that a man found a woman as beautiful as Merideth McCloud naked in his bed. He'd be a fool not to take advantage.

With his gaze on hers, he let his finger drift downward over skin that was as soft and cool as the satin sheet clutched at her breasts. When he bumped against the taut edge of the sheet, he curled his finger around the fabric between her breasts. "Come here," he commanded, his voice husky.

The graze of his knuckle against Merideth's bare skin was like a flint striking stone, igniting the flammable trail he'd left on her chest. Heat quickly spread through her body, racing to every limb. She saw the same heat flame in John Lee's eyes. She wanted him, she realized with a suddenness that left her breathless. More than any man she'd ever known. And unlike the last time, when he'd caught her unaware, this time she was in control and she would have him. She dipped her face lower over his, smiling seductively. "What?" she whispered.

In answer, he raised his head and caught her lower lip between his teeth. At the same time, he gave the sheet a sharp tug, ripping it from beneath her arms. She tossed back her head and covered her breasts with her hands, laughing as cool air hit her bare skin.

"Come here. I'll warm you up." Curling an arm around her neck, he drew her to him while with his other hand he guided her body over his.

As he promised, the heat was there to warm her. Mouth to mouth, chest to breast, thigh to thigh. That their bodies fit so perfectly together registered only fleetingly in Merideth's mind before other impressions took over...the strongest being the length of maleness growing hard at the juncture of her legs. An ache grew deep inside her, and she shifted, rubbing against him, trying to ease it.

He groaned at the seductive pressure, the sound vibrating against her lips and her breasts and echoing deep inside her. Gathering her hair from her face, he brought his hands together at the nape of her neck, then drew away far enough to look at her. "That mirror sure would come in handy right now."

The regret in his voice drew a smile. "How so?"

He tipped back his head and stared forlornly at the ceiling. "If it wasn't covered up, I wouldn't have to imagine how good your backside looks naked. I could see it."

Chuckling, Merideth nipped at his chin. "Oh, poor baby."

He shifted his gaze to hers again and sighed. "I guess I'll just have to rely on my sense of touch."

Even as he said it, he released her hair, letting it fall once again to curtain her face, and aligned the tips of his fingers along her spine. Roughened from years of working with his bare hands, his fingers traced the nubby length of her spine. The rasp of his fingers against her flesh was like sandpaper on silk and sent every nerve in her body quivering. She arched, throwing back her head, the ache inside her growing, tightening into a hard knot of desire.

"You like that, do you?" he murmured, watching her eyes heat as he teased the flesh in the curve of her lower back.

"Yes," she whispered, then groaned when he slid his hands over her bottom and cupped her cheeks in his palms, pressing her hard against him. "Oh, yes," she sighed, lowering her gaze to his. Recognizing the need in his eyes as the same that twisted inside her, she pushed her hands against his chest and sat up, straddling him. One by one she plucked his shirt's buttons from their holes, then gave a tug, pulling the shirt's tail from the waist of his pants. With the palms of her hands, she swept the fabric back, baring his chest to her hungry gaze.

Tanned from hours spent working beneath a Texas sun, his skin stretched taut over well-defined muscle. Dragging a finger down his chest and onto the smooth plane of his abdomen, she counted one...two...three.... A six-pack, she thought with a lusty sigh. And all tall-boys.

He flinched as her fingers trailed lower, and she smiled. "Ticklish?" she teased.

"Would you stop if I said yes?"

"Maybe."

He grinned wickedly. "Then, no, I'm not ticklish." Lifting a hand, he cupped a full breast. "Are you?"

"No."

As if to prove her wrong, he raked a thumb over her nipple and she sucked in a breath as the sweetest sensations spun slowly downward from her breast to settle low in her abdomen like warm, thick honey. That she wanted him didn't surprise her. That she could want him so desperately, did.

Melting against him, she pressed her lips against his. "Make love to me, John Lee," she whispered.

"Sugar," he murmured, "it would be my pleasure." Rolling, he flipped her to her back, reversing their positions, and planted his hands on either side of her head to hold himself over her. Lowering his face, he warmed her lips with his breath, then covered her mouth with his. He drank deeply, greedily, probing her mouth with his tongue, teasing her, stoking the fire that blazed within her until she was writhing beneath him. She arched, reaching for him, her nipples grazing his chest, the mound of her femininity thrusting hard against his groin.

Tearing his mouth from hers, he slid his lips over her chin and down the smooth column of her throat. He cupped a breast, tipping the nipple to his mouth. He licked, sucked, soothed while he moved his hand down her abdomen, kneading her tense stomach muscles, then closed it over her mound. She bucked, arching high against the pressure, crying out his name.

In her entire life Merideth had never felt so utterly exposed, so out of control. Like a wild woman, she clawed at his shirt, ripping it from his shoulders, wanting him as naked as she. She raked her nails down his back, marking him, then dove her fingers below the waist of his jeans, desperate to rid him of them.

Every touch of her flesh against his, every frustrated whimper that escaped her lips, pushed John Lee closer and closer to the edge. What had been a simple promise to pleasure her, suddenly turned to a blinding need to possess her. He had to have her, had to feel every inch of her bare skin rubbing seductively against his, had to feel her velvet softness close around him. Balancing himself with one hand, he reached for his buckle and, with her help, quickly freed himself of his jeans.

"Merideth." Her name was half warning, half plea as he moved over her, covering her body with his. Perspiration already slicked their skins and heat rose between them, welding their bodies together, but John Lee had to know that there would be no regrets. Filling his hands with her hair, he forced her face to his. The eyes that met his were wild, glazed with passion. "Are you sure this is what you want?"

"Yes," she whispered. "Yes, please."

Stretching a hand to the nightstand, John Lee withdrew a foil packet, quickly opened it, and slipped the needed protection in place.

Impatient, Meredith reached for him, drawing his face to hers. Their tongues mated, their breaths burned and the heat climbed higher. He shifted, placing a hand between them, separating the folds that hid her feminine opening, and guided himself to her. She arched at the first contact, dragging her lips from his. "Oh, please," she begged. "Please."

With a single thrust, he was inside her, her hot, moist, feminine walls closing around him. The pleasure was so sharp, so mind-shattering, he froze, his chest heaving. Pressing his forehead against hers, he drew in a long, shuddering breath, fighting for control, needing it to prolong this exquisite pleasure. When he was sure he'd won it, he began to move, slowly at first, setting the rhythm, then increasing the speed, the intensity, until they were racing together as one.

He could feel the tension in her building, hear her desperate cries for release at his ear. Hooking an arm behind her back, he rose to his knees, bringing her up with him, and guided her legs around his waist. With his broad hands braced at her hips, he thrust one last time, and buried himself deeply inside her, holding her against him. The explosion was simultaneous, a blast of heat and sensation that had them holding tight to each other to keep from shattering.

Trembling, John Lee fell forward, bracing a hand on the bed. He rolled to his back, holding Merideth tight against his chest, while the aftershocks of her climax continued to pulse around him.

With a sigh, she snuggled against him, burying her nose in his neck. ''If I'd only known...''

In spite of his weakened state, he chuckled. ''Sugar, I've been trying to tell you. You just weren't listening.''

Six

Merideth awakened slowly to the sound of the shower running and John Lee singing, slightly off-key. The song was a familiar one George Strait had put on the charts about a love between a young girl and boy and a note that said Check Yes Or No. Though John Lee was crucifying the lyrics, changing some words and humming others, she liked the song's story...and she liked the man singing it.

She smiled as memories from the night before drifted slowly through her mind like lazy clouds across a clear summer sky. Smoothing a hand across the sheet at her side, she found the lingering warmth from his body and curled her hand into a fist as if to capture it. With a sigh, she drew the fist to her breasts, holding it there.

She couldn't remember ever being made love to so thoroughly, so completely...so passionately. Even thinking about it sent a rush of warmth spreading through her body. She pushed her face against the pillow, inhaling deeply, filling her senses with scents of John Lee and the lingering ones of their lovemaking.

How could she feel so utterly sated and yet yearn for him at the same time? Could she be falling in love with him? Shocked by the thought, she rolled to her back, pushing her hair from her face. *Love?* She stared wide-eyed at the ceiling and the folds of shimmering gold fabric gathered there, testing the word.

A shiver of apprehension chased through her and she pulled the sheet to her chin. She'd never been in love before. Granted, she'd had lovers, some of whom she cared for deeply. But she'd never given her heart to a man. Not even Marcus, the man she'd lived with, created a child with. For years, she'd thought she'd inherited her father's cold heart and was incapable of love.

Hesitantly, she crossed her hands over her heart, feeling its fluttering beat beneath her palms. There was something there now, though, she realized, some emotion, almost like an ache, that she'd never experienced before.

Could it be love? she asked herself again. Could she be falling in love with John Lee?

She gave herself a firm shake, dismissing the notion as ridiculous. A person didn't just suddenly fall in love with a man they'd known all their life! Besides, she and John Lee were ill-suited. He was beer to her champagne, denim to her silk. A macho-jock-turned-cowboy, that's what he was. And Merideth preferred her men with a little more polish, a little more class.

So how was she to explain this sudden yearning for him? Was it simply lust?

At that moment, the bathroom door opened, and John Lee stepped into the room, bringing with him a cloud of steam and the clean scent of bath soap and shaving cream. Wrapped low on his hips he wore a towel which gaped just a bit on one leg, exposing a muscled thigh and a jagged scar over his knee. He held another towel at his head, rubbing water from his hair. Muscles bunched and corded along his arm, and his pecs swelled, forming almost perfect squares of muscle on the wall of his chest. He stopped when his gaze met hers and dropped the towel to his side, a smile slowly curving his lips.

"Good mornin'."

At his husky greeting, Merideth released a breath she wasn't aware she'd been holding. Lust, she told herself. Yes, it must be lust if just looking at him made her go all soft and warm inside. He was without a doubt the most devilishly handsome, the most incredibly sexy man she'd ever laid eyes on.

Returning his smile, she smoothed her hands across her breasts, straightening the sheet. "Good morning," she murmured almost shyly. "Did you sleep well?"

Catching an end of the towel in each hand, he strode toward the bed, mischief in his eyes and in his step. "You ought to know the answer to that question as well as I do." When he reached the side of the bed, he sank a knee on the mattress beside her and leaned over, flipping the towel behind her head. With a tug he drew her to her knees in front of him. "But who needs sleep when there's a beautiful woman around?" Dipping his head, he closed his mouth over hers.

His lips were cool, his flavor minty and the scents that drifted around her were all musky male. She sighed, looping her arms around his neck, and melted against him. How does he do this? she wondered fleetingly. How can he turn me to putty with one look, one kiss?

She quickly dismissed the thought as unimportant. The

fact was, he *could*—and she was going to enjoy every minute of it.

When he deepened the kiss, she tangled her fingers in the damp, sandy-blond hair at his neck and clung to him. Yes, she thought with a breathy sigh, she could definitely get used to this.

The phone beside the bed rang, startling Merideth. She tried to pull away to answer it, but John Lee took another turn with the towel, wrapping it around his wrist and taking up the slack. "Let it ring," he told her, holding her in place. "If it's important, they'll call back." He dipped his head again, intending to finish what he'd started, but Merideth ducked out from under his arms.

"We can't just let it ring," she scolded him as she crawled for the bedside table. "It might be something important."

With her bare bottom turned up to him, John Lee couldn't resist. He whipped the towel into a rope, then released one end, and gave it a quick snap just as Merideth picked up the receiver.

"Ouch!" she yelped, clapping a hand to the sting on her bottom. Glaring at him over her shoulder, she pulled the receiver to her ear. "Carter residence," she snapped peevishly.

"Hi, Mrs. Baker," a female voice drawled from the other end of the line. "John Lee was supposed to come over for breakfast this morning, but he never showed up. Is he there?"

Being mistaken for Mrs. Baker was insulting enough, but the sexy pout in the woman's voice and her announcement that John Lee was supposed to be having breakfast with her made every muscle in Merideth's body turn to stone. There was no question in Merideth's mind what the bimbo was planning to serve for breakfast! With her eyes locked on John Lee's face, she tried to keep her expression schooled, her voice calm. "May I tell him who's calling?" she asked sweetly.

She listened, then replied, "Yes, hold on a minute and I'll get him." Tightening her fingers around the receiver, she pulled it from her ear, then reared back and threw it as hard as she could at John Lee, aiming below his waist.

Instinctively, he covered himself with his hands and the phone cracked against his knuckles and dropped at his knees. "What the hell did you do that for?" he demanded angrily.

Merideth flounced from the bed, and turned, her chin tipped high enough to catch water. "I wouldn't keep *Muffy* waiting, if I were you," she warned him, then turned and stormed to the bathroom, slamming and locking the door behind her.

Doubled over, Merideth braced her hands against the marble vanity in the master bathroom and dragged in a ragged breath. How could she have been so foolish? So stupid? So blind? She'd known John Lee Carter all her life! She knew what a playboy he was, how much he enjoyed women. She'd seen all the pictures of the women on his walls. She was the one who had ripped them all off! Yet, knowing this, she'd slept with him, made love with him, even fantasized a moment about being in love with him.

A knifelike pain, very much like the one she'd suffered when she'd learned she'd lost her baby, tore through her heart and she pressed a hand at her breasts to keep her chest from splitting wide open. Tears filled her eyes and she sucked in another ragged breath, trying to hold them back.

Oh, God, why does it hurt so much? she cried silently.

You hurt because you love him.

The answer came out of thin air and drew her up short. Love him? John Lee? She gulped back the tears, ready to argue, but slowly realized that, yes, it was true. Her feelings weren't just a fantasy, her attraction to him not simply lust. They were real. Real enough to cause her pain.

She lifted her head and stared at her reflection in the bathroom mirror, numbed by the realization. But how could she have fallen in love with him? she asked herself in bewilderment. When?

She strained, trying to remember every detail of the last few weeks, sorting through her emotions for clues as to when her feelings for him had changed. But she couldn't put her finger on any one event, any one moment. She just knew that she loved him.

And at the moment, the man she was in love with was in the other room, talking to some bimbo named Muffy on the phone.

Anger burned through Merideth. Of all the nerve! Cuddling up with her while knowing full well that he had another woman in town waiting for him. Merideth knew she was selfish, that she'd really never learned the basic principles of sharing that other people mastered as early as kindergarten, but this was asking too much!

Damn him for making me fall in love with him! she raged silently. And damn him for his playboy ways!

She straightened, whisking the heels of her hands beneath her eyes, wiping away the tears. She wouldn't be just another filly in his stable of willing women, she told herself. She was a McCloud, after all, she had the McCloud pride. And a McCloud never accepted anything in parts. It was all, or nothing.

She squared her shoulders. Well, she could fall out of

love as quickly as she'd fallen in. It was just a matter of setting her mind to it, of setting her heart against him.

It was all a matter of control.

"Women," John Lee muttered under his breath. "Who needs 'em?" He lifted a fifty-pound bag of feed from the dock and hefted it to his shoulder. He wobbled a second, his bad knee balking at the added strain.

Usually he sent a couple of his men to pick up feed when the ranch's supply was running low, but today John Lee had been so desperate to get out of the house and away from Merideth, he'd elected to go himself.

He was sick and damned tired of the icy silence he'd lived with ever since Muffy had called, and suffering a little pain in his knee had seemed a small price to pay in order to escape it for a while.

And he'd suffer, all right. He could already feel his knee swelling.

The hell of it was, he didn't know what he'd done to deserve Merideth's ire. He suspected it had to do with the call from Muffy, since he could date the silence to almost that precise moment. But when he'd tried to question Merideth about it, she refused to talk to him.

Was it possible that she was jealous? Though the idea that she might be rather pleased him, he quickly dismissed it as an impossibility. Jealousy and Merideth just didn't seem to go hand-in-hand.

Not liking the icy shoulder she turned to him every time he got near her, he'd tried his best to get back in her good graces. Hell, he'd even hired a painter to paint Cassie's room, thinking that would please her! But she hadn't said a word to him when the job was completed. She'd simply accepted his generosity as if it was her due.

"Women," he growled and ducked his head, striding

angrily for his truck. "A royal pain in the butt, if you ask me."

"What are you mumbling about, John Lee?"

He snapped his head up to see Jesse Barrister, Merideth's brother-in-law, standing at the rear of his truck. "Women," he muttered again, only louder this time. He shouldered the bag of feed onto the pile on the bed of his truck, then whacked his palms against his thighs to shake off the dust they'd left there. "How can you stand being married to one?" he asked Jesse. "And having one under foot all the time?"

Jesse hooked a boot on the truck's bumper, biting back a smile. "Oh, it's a hardship, all right. Home-cooked meals, a sweet young thing to cuddle up with at night, someone to talk to when I'm lonely." He chuckled. "But I manage as best I can."

John Lee grunted. He couldn't argue the meals. He honestly hadn't thought Merideth could cook, but over the last couple of weeks, she'd been spreading some pretty fair grub on the table for him and his men. But as to cuddling up with her—well, forget that! These days, trying to cuddle up with Merideth was like trying to cuddle up to a porcupine. Every time he got within a foot of her, she turned her back and shot him full of barbs from that sharp tongue of hers.

"Eatin' regular's all right, I guess," he admitted grudgingly. "Though a man can hire that done."

"Yeah, and I suppose a man could pay for the other, if he had a mind to."

"I wouldn't know," John Lee said, his chest swelling a bit, as he gave a manly hitch to his belt. "I've never had to. But if I ever did," he added, leveling a frown on Jesse, "I guaran-damn-tee you I'd a lot sooner fork over some cash than I would my name. At least I could go home afterwards, and not have my eyebrows singed off or suffer frostbite, depending on the woman's mood.''

Chuckling, Jesse seemed to decide a change of subject might be wise. He one-knuckled his hat to the back of his head and braced his arms over his raised knee. ''Finally got a look at that niece of yours. She sure is a pretty thing.''

At the mention of Cassie, John Lee's chest puffed again, but with pride this time. ''She's a sweet one, all right, and as good-natured as a cocker spaniel pup.''

Jesse cocked his head, his look skeptical. ''Couldn't prove it by me. When I left, she was raising the roof. Man, that girl's got a set of lungs! Had Mandy and Merideth both running around like chickens with their heads cut off, trying to find something to please her.''

John Lee frowned. ''Merideth has Cassie over at the Double-Cross?''

Jesse nodded. ''Yeah. Came right after lunch for her cooking lesson.''

Cooking lesson? John Lee scowled. So that's how Merideth was pulling off all those home-cooked meals. Mandy was helping her. He should have known.

''Though there's not much cooking going on,'' Jessie added, ''not with Cassie fretting the way she was. Can't imagine what's ailing her.''

Paling, John Lee braced a hand against the side of the truck, his knees going weak. ''Cassie's sick?''

Jesse lifted a shoulder as he dragged his boot from the bumper. ''Beats me. Didn't look sick.'' He laid a finger over the brim of his hat, tugging it back down to shade his eyes. '''Course, I don't have much experience with babies.'' Giving the brim a final tap, he added slyly, ''Although Mandy and I are doing what we can to change that.''

As far as John Lee was concerned, they could mate like rabbits. He was too worried about Cassie to care. He hadn't known she was sick. Of course, he'd left the house that morning before she or Merideth were up, but she'd seemed fine the night before when he'd checked on her before turning in.

"If you ask me, Merideth is the one who looks sick."

John Lee's head whipped around. "Merideth is sick?" he repeated.

"Haven't you noticed those dark circles under her eyes? Pale as a ghost, too. In fact, she looks as bad as when Mandy and Sam first brought her home to the Double-Cross." He wagged his head sorrowfully. "Mandy kept trying to get her to lie down and rest and let her take care of Cassie for a while, but Merideth wouldn't have any of that. You couldn't pry that baby off of her with a crowbar. She's that crazy about the girl."

John Lee swallowed hard. Yeah, Merideth was crazy about Cassie, all right, and Cassie about her. He'd seen proof enough of that. But he hadn't known Merideth was sick. He hadn't noticed any dark circles, or any other symptoms for that matter. But, then again, they'd both been doing a pretty good job of avoiding each other.

Guilt settled on his shoulders. If she was sick, it was his fault. She was accustomed to being pampered and waited on, not working like a scullery maid from dawn till dusk, managing a house and cooking meals while taking care of a baby. And what had he done to help her? Nothin'. He hadn't lifted so much as a finger, other than to play with Cassie when he was home, which wasn't all that much help, really.

He had to get to Merideth, he told himself, to Cassie, and see for himself that they were okay. "Are they still at the Double-Cross?" he asked.

Jesse shook his head. "I doubt it. Heard Merideth saying something about taking Cassie home and seeing if she wouldn't be happier in her own bed."

John Lee spun and headed for his truck.

"John Lee!"

"What?" he called over his shoulder.

"Aren't you going to load the rest of your feed?"

John Lee tore open the door, slammed it shut behind him, then stuck his head out the window as he gunned the engine. "Tell Bud I'll send one of the boys for it later," he yelled. Ducking back inside, he tore out of the parking lot, taking the turn onto the highway on two wheels. Sacks of feed flew off the bed of the truck and busted open on the pavement, scattering grain across the road.

Jesse stared after the truck. "Well, I'll be a son of a gun," he muttered. "Mandy may be right about those two." Wagging his head in wonder, he turned for the feed store to deliver John Lee's message to Bud.

John Lee hit the back door at a full run. "Merideth!" he yelled. "Where are you?" He paused, listening, and his blood iced when he heard Cassie's screams. His heart battering like a jackhammer against his chest, he busted through the kitchen door, and ran for the master bedroom.

Inside the nursery, he found Merideth pacing while frantically patting at Cassie's back. When she turned, he saw that her eyes were red and puffy, and tears streaked her cheeks. His heart nearly breaking, he crossed to her, reaching for Cassie. "Merideth, sugar—here, let me take her."

She twisted away from him, tightening her arms around Cassie, refusing to let her go. "No!" she sobbed, then grabbed for his arm, clamping a hand around it. He winced when her nails bit into his flesh. "Oh, John Lee," she wailed, "she won't stop crying. I've tried every-thing." Releasing him, she cupped the hand tenderly at the back of Cassie's head. "Shhh," she soothed, then hiccuped a sob herself. "It's o-okay, darling. Just p-please tell Merideth what's wrong."

If John Lee thought his heart was breaking before, he was wrong, because at that moment it split wide open. Emotion burned through him and stung the back of his throat. He couldn't stand to see his girls in such misery. Knowing he'd never convince Merideth to let Cassie go, he scooped them both up into his arms and sat down in the rocking chair. He shifted Merideth across his lap, pulling her head to his shoulder while she continued to clutch Cassie to her breasts.

"Now calm down, sugar," he soothed, "and tell me what's been going on."

Merideth shuddered and dragged a wrist beneath her eyes. "It started last night," she began as she stroked Cassie's hair, never once taking her eyes off the child. "She woke up crying. I thought she was hungry, so I gave her a bottle and she went back to sleep. Then shortly after you left this morning, she woke up again. She felt warm, so I gave her some of that pediatric fever medicine I found in your medicine cabinet. That helped for a while, but then she started crying again and the fever returned." Fresh tears welled in her eyes. "I didn't know what to do, so I took her to Mandy's. Mandy insists that nothing's wrong with her, that she's either teething or has a touch of colic. But Cassie won't stop crying, and she's still running a fever." She tipped her face to his, tears streak-ing down her cheeks. "She's going to be okay, isn't she? Please tell me that she is."

Seeing the fear in her eyes, John Lee knew she must

be remembering losing her son. He tightened his arms around her and pressed his lips to her forehead. "She's going to be fine," he assured her. "We'll call the doctor, tell him what's going on, and see what he says."

John Lee leaned over the bed and brushed the hair from Merideth's forehead. Seeing the dark circles Jesse had mentioned, he pressed a kiss on each one. Though she stirred, she didn't wake.

He reached across her to lay a hand against Cassie's forehead. Even after all the doctor's assurances that Cassie was just suffering from a severe case of teething, Merideth had refused to put her in her crib, but had insisted on taking her to bed with her. Even now, her body curved around Cassie's, forming a physical shield for her, protecting her, even in sleep.

Straightening, John Lee removed his hand from Cassie's forehead, letting out a sigh of relief. Cool as a cucumber, he concluded. The fever was gone. He only hoped Merideth would recover as quickly. Though the doctor had found nothing medically wrong with her, he had ordered her to rest, attributing her paleness, the listlessness in her eyes to exhaustion.

When he'd made his diagnosis, that guilt John Lee had experienced earlier while talking to Jesse had eaten a little deeper into his soul. Drawing a chair to the side of the bed, he caught Merideth's hand in his, weaving his fingers through hers as he watched her sleep.

"I'll take care of you," he promised in a low whisper. "And I'll get Mrs. Baker back over here so she can do the cooking and cleaning again, even if I have to hog-tie her to do it." He sucked in a shuddery breath, squeezing her hand between his. "I'll even take down that dang mirror, if it'll make you happy."

As far as sacrifices went, it wasn't much, but considering John Lee's affection for the mirror, in his mind at least, it ranked right up there with offering her one of his limbs.

"Now, I don't want her upset," John Lee warned Mrs. Baker the next morning as he guided her into the kitchen. "The doctor says she needs rest and I intend to see that she gets it."

Mrs. Baker plopped her purse down on the kitchen counter, then sniffed, folding her hands at her waist. "Rest, my foot. What she needs is to change her cheating ways."

John Lee hauled in a breath, fighting for patience. "That kind of attitude is exactly what I'm referring to," he said firmly, "and I better not hear you talking like that in front of Merideth."

Mrs. Baker lifted her chin. "Somebody needs to set her straight. Running around on her husband, taking money from men for pleasuring them. And now moving in here with you. No telling what kind of influence she's having on that poor innocent baby." She sniffed again, a sure sign of her disapproval. "She's nothing but a tramp and has ruined more lives than I care to count. I just don't want her ruining yours, too."

Confused, John Lee stared. "What in the world are you talking about? Merideth doesn't have a husband and she sure as hell isn't selling herself to any men."

Snatching an apron from the hook on the back of the pantry door, Mrs. Baker whipped it around her waist. "She most certainly does have a husband. A highly respected man in the community, and a good doctor, too."

John Lee thunked a hand against his head, to clear his brain. Someone in the room was crazy, and he was pretty sure it wasn't him. "Mrs. Baker," he began patiently. "Merideth isn't married to a doctor. In fact, she's never been married."

"Humph! I see she's got you fooled, too. Putting on wigs and changing her clothes. She even changes her name so no one will recognize her. Monique, Charise, and now Merideth. She pretends that she's got a mental problem, some sort of personality disorder, but she's just using that as an excuse so she can go about her wild ways. Oh, she's a slick one," she warned, shaking a finger at John Lee, "don't say I didn't warn you."

A lightbulb flashed on in John Lee's head. *Monique. Charise.* Those were the names of the characters Merideth played on that soap opera she starred in. The same show that Mrs. Baker watched religiously every day. He vaguely remembered Merideth telling him about Monique and her alter ego Charise, the high-class prostitute, but he'd been so absorbed in Merideth herself at the time that he hadn't really paid that much attention.

And Mrs. Baker, God love her befuddled head, thought all those characters on that show were real people, and that Merideth was really Monique. He squeezed his forehead between the width of his hand. He'd laugh if it wasn't all so damn sad.

Dropping his hand to his side, he sighed wearily. As he looked at Mrs. Baker and the determined set of her jaw, he knew his work was cut out for him. Taking his housekeeper by the elbow, he gently guided her to the table. "Have a seat, Mrs. Baker. We need to have a little talk."

"She *what!*"

"Shhh," John Lee warned in a whisper. "I don't want

her to know that I told you. It'd just embarrass her even more.''

Merideth sank back against the pillow, staring at John Lee in dismay. ''She's crazy! Everybody knows that the characters on that show are fictitious. Even the town where the story is set is a product of some screenwriter's imagination.''

Her eyes widened even more as the full implications of the mistaken identity soaked in. ''And how could she possibly believe that I'm anything like Monique! Even on her best days Monique is a psychiatrist's nightmare! And Charise is nothing but a—''

The word *prostitute* died on her lips and her mouth sagged open as she realized that Mrs. Baker thought *she* was the prostitute. She remembered the look on Mrs. Baker's face the morning she'd caught Merideth and John Lee in bed kissing, and later when Mrs. Baker had called her a tramp.

That memory was quickly followed by another, the look of hatred on Mrs. Baker's face the first night they'd met when John Lee had invited Merideth over for dinner. If looks could kill, Merideth knew she wouldn't be alive today. At the time, she'd wondered what she'd done to earn such disapproval, but in retrospect she could almost understand Mrs. Baker's condemning look. The woman had thought that John Lee was bringing a prostitute into his home to care for his orphaned niece!

Merideth pressed her lips together, her anger giving way to amusement as she began to see the humor in the situation. Merideth McCloud a prostitute! What a hoot! She started to laugh. Softly at first, nothing more than a chuckle really, but the more she thought about it, the funnier it seemed. Her amusement grew until she was laughing so hard she could barely catch her breath.

John Lee hopped up and down beside the bed, flapping his hands, trying to get her to quieten down, fearing Mrs. Baker would hear her. But Merideth laughed even harder. Finally, he climbed onto the bed and clapped a hand over her mouth. "For God's sake, Merideth, get a grip!" he whispered loudly.

Though he succeeded in smothering the sound of her laughter, he could still see the amusement in her eyes. Not sure he could trust her to keep quiet, he narrowed an eye at her. "Do you think you can control yourself now?" At her nod, he withdrew his hand.

"I'm sorry," she whispered, trying her darnedest not to laugh any more. "But the idea of Mrs. Baker thinking that I'm a prostitute is just too funny."

John Lee collapsed on the bed beside her in frustration. "Well, she did. In fact, I had a hell of a time convincing her that you weren't. She didn't want to accept the fact that the show and all its characters are nothing but make-believe." He cocked his head to look at her, his mouth puckered in a frown. "Do you know she's been watching that soap opera for almost thirty years?" He wagged his head. "After that long a time, I guess the characters would seem almost real to her."

Sober now, Merideth nodded her agreement. "The studio does receive some rather strange fan mail. I remember one letter in particular from a woman who had cancer. She wanted to know if an appointment could be arranged for her with Dr. Kline, my character's husband. There was an episode," she explained, "where he cured another character of cancer and this lady hoped he could cure her, as well. Anyway, the director read it on the set one day during a break, and everyone had a good laugh." She turned to look at John Lee. "But it doesn't seem so funny any more. In fact, it's really kind of sad."

John Lee wrapped an arm around her shoulder and drew her to his side. "Yeah, I know what you mean. Just look at poor old Mrs. Baker. She doesn't have any family to speak of, and has lived alone for as long as I can remember. Those soaps she watches are company for her, and I guess over the years she's gotten so involved in the characters' lives that she's let that fine line between fiction and fact kind of fade a bit."

Merideth dipped her head and plucked at a loose thread on her nightgown's sleeve. After a moment, she said softly, "I'll be nicer to her."

John Lee gave her a tight squeeze. "Now don't go thinkin' I told you all this just so you'd feel sorry for her."

Merideth laid her head on his shoulder, accepting his comfort. "I don't. It's just that after walking in her shoes for the last couple of weeks, I have a new appreciation for her."

If she'd offered to adopt Mrs. Baker as her own mother, John Lee wouldn't have been any more surprised. He looked down at the top of her head, wondering what had come over her. "Really?"

"She works so hard," Merideth murmured, staring at the thread as she rolled it between her fingers. "Cooking for you and your men and keeping this big house clean is a full-time job. I don't know how she managed to do it and care for Cassie, too. I certainly did a lousy job of it and I'm a great deal younger than Mrs. Baker."

John Lee gave her another squeeze. "Awww, now. You've carried on just fine."

Merideth shot him a dubious look. "You must have forgotten about those sandwiches."

He chuckled. "No, I haven't forgotten and I bet my men haven't, either. All those tiny little squares and those fussy little carrot curls. Shoot, we didn't know whether to eat 'em or frame 'em.''

Merideth smiled sheepishly, remembering the stunned look on the men's faces when she'd placed the platter in front of them. "They were rather ridiculous, weren't they?''

John Lee settled himself more comfortably at her side. "Nah, sugar. They were just a surprise, is all. In fact, I think the men might miss that special little touch you've added to their meals now that Mrs. Baker will be taking over the cooking again.''

Merideth looked at him curiously. "What special touch?''

"Oh, the linen napkins, the sprigs of parsley on the side of their plates. In fact, they're liable to rebel if Mrs. Baker doesn't carve the butter into those cute little flowers for them like you did.''

Merideth pursed her lips, frowning. "You're making fun of me.''

He pressed a hand at his chest, looking wounded. "Would I do a thing like that?''

Though she tried not to smile, she found it hard to resist John Lee's boyish charm. She gave him a nudge with her shoulder. "Don't you have cows to punch or something?''

Grinning, he shifted to his side, curling his body around hers. "Or something," he said suggestively and let his gaze drop to her mouth.

Merideth recognized that look in his eye, and though she'd accepted the comfort of his arm, was even grateful for it, she wasn't sure she could trust herself if he got any closer. "John Lee," she warned. "Don't you dare. The doctor might have been wrong. I may have something contagious.''

He just grinned at her and covered her hand with his, holding it against his heart. ''I'll take my chances.'' He leaned closer, pinning her against the headboard, and brushed her lips with his, once, twice, three times, then nipped at her lower lip before finally closing his mouth over hers.

With her hand pressed beneath his and against the familiar warmth of his chest, she felt the quickening of his heartbeat, the tightening of muscle as he deepened the kiss. There wasn't a man alive who could kiss like John Lee Carter, who could scatter a woman's thoughts with the flick of his tongue.

She could feel herself falling, slipping deeper and deeper under his seductive spell. She knew she had to stop him while she still had the power to do so. Slipping her fingers between their lips, she firmly, if regretfully, separated herself from him.

Surprised, John Lee lifted his gaze to hers. ''What?''

''No,'' she told him softly.

''No, what?'' he asked in confusion.

Tears burned and Merideth quickly pulled the covers over her shoulder and rolled to her side, turning her back on John Lee. ''The first time was a mistake, John Lee,'' she murmured, trying to keep the tears from her voice. ''Let's don't make it again.''

Seven

John Lee rolled from the bed and to his feet in one smooth move, then had to grab for the mattress when his bad knee refused to take his weight. "Mistake!" he yelled, forcing himself to a standing position. "And where, may I ask, was the mistake in us making love?"

Merideth caught her lip between her teeth at the hurt she heard in his voice. She didn't want to hurt him. But she didn't want him to hurt her, either. And one of them was bound to get hurt if she allowed this to continue. Better to end it now, while there was a chance they could still be friends.

She closed her eyes, gathering her emotions deeply inside herself, not wanting him to see the lie behind the performance she was about to give. When she was sure she was in control, she feigned a sigh, then rolled over and sat up, fluffing her hair.

"There was nothing *wrong* with your abilities," she

assured him, "if that's what you're concerned about."
She cocked her head and smiled coyly. "In fact, I rather
enjoyed our little tryst. But in all fairness, John Lee, for
us to even consider an affair is ludicrous."

He had swelled at the word *tryst,* but exploded at the
word *ludicrous.* "Ludicrous!" he roared, his face flush-
ing an angry red. "And what is ludicrous about us having
an affair?"

She drew a delicate hand to her throat and looked at
him in surprise, though she was dying inside. "Why, I'd
think that's obvious." She opened her hand, gesturing
toward him. "You're a cowboy, a man who enjoys the
simple things in life, while I—" she pointed gracefully
at herself "—prefer a more cosmopolitan life-style. Oil
and water. We simply don't mix."

John Lee sucked in a furious breath. "Well, excuse me
for differing with you, Miss High-and-Mighty McCloud,
but I thought we mixed just fine." He yanked his hat
from the foot of the bed and rammed it on his head. "But
now that you've brought it to my attention, I can see that
you were right. We don't mix. In fact, I wonder how I
stomached kissing you at all, much less making love to
you."

Staring at the door John Lee had slammed behind him,
Merideth heaved a long shuddery breath and let the mask
she'd assumed drop, releasing all the emotions she'd kept
locked up inside. Regret rose, clogging her throat, stinging her eyes. With her lips trembling uncontrollably, she
drew a pillow across her raised knees and fisted her hands
in its softness.

She wouldn't cry, she told herself. If she did, she was
afraid she'd never be able to stop.

She tried to tell herself that she'd done the right thing,

that a confrontation was inevitable and that she was wise to put an end to the relationship before one of them was hurt. But for some reason, she didn't find comfort in her reassurances. What she wanted, needed, was John Lee. She wanted to call him back, to take back the lies she'd told him. She wanted to curl up against his side again with his arm wrapped around her. She wanted to feel the comforting warmth of his body next to hers. She wanted to laugh and tease with him. She wanted to feel the pressure of his lips on hers, to experience again that dizzying loss of control.

She wanted to pretend those other women didn't exist.

A whimper from the nursery interrupted her thoughts. Tossing aside the pillow, she swung her legs over the edge of the bed and hurried across the room, pulling on her robe.

Cassie was sitting up in her crib and when she saw Merideth, she lifted her arms, her chin quivering.

"Hey there, sweetheart," Merideth whispered as she scooped her from the crib. "How are you feeling?"

More asleep than awake, Cassie snuggled against Merideth's neck and rubbed sleepily at her eyes. "You shouldn't be waking up yet," Merideth scolded gently. She laid a hand on the baby's cheek, thinking the fever had returned and that was what had awakened her, but was relieved to find the cheek cool to her touch. She started to lay Cassie back down so she could finish her nap, but when she did, Cassie clung to Merideth, whimpering.

Knowing full well she was spoiling her, Merideth drew her back into her arms, crossed to the rocker and sat down. Pushing a bare foot against the carpet, she set the rocker in motion, needing Cassie's comforting warmth as much as Cassie obviously needed to be held.

Burying her nose in Cassie's soft, downy hair, she closed her eyes and smiled a watery smile. A month ago she hadn't been able to touch Cassie, much less hold her. Her grief over the loss of her son wouldn't allow her to. But Cassie, in her innocence, had helped heal her heart. Merideth only hoped that she'd been able to fill the void in Cassie's life as well.

With a sigh, she pressed her lips to Cassie's head, then drew back to look at her. That angelic face with its cute button nose and the eyes that were so much like John Lee's. As Merideth watched, Cassie's lids grew heavier and heavier until finally she closed her eyes and snuggled closer, burrowing against Merideth's breasts, her tiny hand still fisted in Merideth's robe. Merideth closed her hand over the fist, her heart swelling.

Oh, how she'd grown to love this precious baby.

John Lee kicked his horse into a lope and headed for the north pasture and the hill beyond that marked his ranch's border. "'Oil and water,' my ass," he muttered darkly, bringing Merideth's words to mind. The wind whipped at his shirt and he rammed his hat a little farther down on his head to keep it from being ripped off his head.

He raced the horse across the pasture, dodging rabbit holes and the occasional scrub of mesquite, and blowing off a little steam. At the bank of a narrow gully, he squeezed his knees at the horse's sides and leaned forward, urging his horse to take the jump. They sailed over the chasm and landed on the opposite side with a scrape of rock and a flurry of dust. Urging his horse on, he rode hard, letting the wind cool his temper and the breakneck speed soothe the dent Merideth had left in his manly pride.

At the top of the hill, he reined the horse in and swung to the ground. Leaving his horse to graze, he stepped out onto the cliff and looked down on Double-Cross land.

Below him lay the spring-fed pond and the slab of limestone where Merideth had lain sunbathing that first day he'd seen her. He hunkered down and plucked a blade of grass to twirl between his fingers, frowning as he stared at the slab of rock.

A country boy. That's what she'd called him, using that as an example of their differences. But if she'd thought she'd offended him by calling him such, she was wrong. John Lee Carter *was* a country boy and damn proud of it. Even during his years in the NFL, when he'd run with some pretty high rollers and received invitations to glamorous parties and exotic locations, he'd never left his boots and hat behind, or the way of life they represented. He was proud of his heritage, comfortable with his image, and damned if he'd change for anyone, including Merideth McCloud.

Oil and water, he thought in disgust, and tossed the shredded blade of grass aside. Well, maybe they were different in some ways, but in the important ones, they fit like the pieces of a jigsaw puzzle. She'd realize that, too, if she ever pulled that snooty nose of hers out of the clouds long enough to give it some real thought.

He plopped down on the ground, drawing up his bad knee to rub at the ache there as he thought over the situation. Something wasn't right, he told himself after a moment's reflection. A woman didn't go from cuddly and sweet to cool indifference in the blink of an eye. Something had to happen to warrant that change. Frowning, he played the entire scene back through his mind in slow motion.

They'd been sitting on the bed, all cuddled up and

talking real friendly-like, he remembered, just before he'd rolled to his side and kissed her. He squinted, trying hard to recall if he'd said anything or done anything that might've set her off, but couldn't think of a dadblasted thing. She'd simply pushed him away with a firm *no*.

He frowned again, his forehead plowing into deep furrows, and looked down at that slab of limestone as if it might hold the answer for him. His thoughts shifted to that first day he'd seen her there, remembering how lost she'd looked, how pitiful…and the sassiness she'd tried to hide it all behind.

Slowly, the furrows smoothed on his forehead. It was an act, he told himself. A full-fledged, Oscar-winning act. She'd wanted that kiss as badly as he had, but for some reason she was pretending that she didn't.

But why?

He pulled off his hat and scratched his head, thinking, and his thoughts carried him back to that morning several weeks back when Muffy had called. He and Merideth had been kissing then, too, and, if John Lee wasn't mistaken—and he considered himself a pretty good judge of such matters—on the verge of making love again, when the phone had rung, interrupting them.

That was when it all started. The coolness, the silence. And if the crisis with Cassie hadn't happened, bringing everything to a head and forcing them to talk, he was sure he'd still be suffering that frigid silence.

He plucked another blade of grass from the ground and clamped it between his teeth. She was jealous, or at least she had been initially. And if a woman was jealous, that usually meant she was interested. If she wasn't, what was the point of getting all puffed up and frosty?

He frowned, studying that notion from a different angle. If a woman showed signs of jealousy, that meant that more than likely she was wanting a more exclusive relationship with a man.

A shudder chased down John Lee's spine at the thought and he pulled the blade of grass from his mouth and tossed it aside before he choked on it.

Exclusive? He swallowed hard. As in him having to give up all his other women? Another shudder shook him and he broke out in a cold sweat. Dragging off his hat, he swiped his arm along his forehead, then slowly settled the hat back on his head.

One woman, he thought, and pressed a hand against his chest, sure that the air was getting thicker, because he was having a hard time drawing a breath.

He couldn't imagine being stuck with one woman the rest of his life, not when there were so many out there. Tall ones and short ones. Curvy ones and slim ones. Redheads and blondes. All of 'em just ripe for the pickin'.

Without meaning to, he let his thoughts drift to Merideth and that long mane of blond hair of hers that he liked tangling his hands in. And those eyes. A clear sparkling blue when she was smiling, but when she was aroused, they changed, darkening and heating to almost indigo. She had a body made for lovin', what with those luscious, sweet-tasting breasts, that tiny waist, and hips that a man could grab ahold of. And that sulky mouth of hers, all moist and pouty, just begging to be kissed...well, hell, a man didn't stand a chance when confronted with all that womanliness!

He groaned and stretched out his leg, rubbing at his knee. But maybe she wasn't jealous, he told himself. After all, it was Merideth he was dealing with. The woman had more moods than ought to be legal and switched 'em so fast a man could get plumb dizzy just trying to keep up. Maybe this was just one of her moods and she was stuck in it a little longer than normal.

He sighed, weary from thinking about it all, and plucked another piece of grass and stuck it between his teeth. So what was he going to do about the situation? he asked himself. Was he going to let her go on pretending she wasn't attracted to him, or was he going to force the issue?

John Lee snatched the blade of grass from his mouth and hopped to his feet. Damned if he was going to let her go on playacting with him! If she didn't want an affair, then by God, she could come right out and say so—and explain her reasons for not wanting to, while she was at it. There wasn't any sense in him sitting around, trying to second-guess her. Who could outguess a woman like Merideth McCloud? And if her answer was still no...well, John Lee could be pretty persuasive when the situation warranted it.

Crossing to his horse, he gathered up his reins and swung up into the saddle, feeling rather pleased with himself.

Life was a whole lot like a football game, he reflected philosophically as he headed his horse for home. A game with opposing players, each with a goal in mind. A person either played the game offensively or defensively, and personally John Lee had always fancied the offensive attack. Pushing toward a goal, trying to outsmart the opposition and gain a little yardage. He knew from experience that throwing a pass, going for the big play, or pushing through a tough defensive line was a whole lot more fun then having to dig in and try and hold a position on the field.

And that's where he'd gone wrong. He hadn't approached this situation with Merideth offensively. He'd been too busy defending. But things were about to change. He chuckled. Yesirree. A little quarterback sneak might be appropriate about now, and if that didn't work, well, there was always the Hail Mary.

Merideth stuffed the last of the wet towels into the dryer and closed the door, then leaned to set the timer. Shoving back a silk sleeve, she reached for the stack of dirty clothes and began to sort out the whites from the colored fabrics and drop them into the washing machine.

While she was in the midst of sorting the clothes, Mrs. Baker walked in, lugging the ironing board. ''What do you think you're doing?'' she fussed as she hung the ironing board on its rack. ''You're supposed to be in bed.''

Merideth bit back a smile at the concern in the woman's voice. ''I'm not sick, Mrs. Baker.''

The housekeeper pursed her lips, but Merideth could see the worry in her eyes, and was touched by it.

''And who said you were?'' she groused gently. She waved a hand, shooing Merideth away. ''Now get on with you. Laundry's my job. Cassie's yours.''

''But she's asleep,'' Merideth complained, tired of being in bed.

''And you should be, too. Doctor's orders. Now scoot! Or John Lee'll have my hide.''

Knowing it would do no good to argue, Merideth turned for the kitchen. Whether she wanted it or not, it seemed she would get the rest the doctor insisted she needed. Little did he know, though, that her exhaustion wasn't a result of overwork, but due to a lack of sleep, and that was all John Lee's fault.

Sighing, she passed through the kitchen, headed for her room. The phone rang, and she called to Mrs. Baker, ''I'll get it!'' then mumbled, ''Unless of course you think I'm too weak to pick up the phone.''

Biting back a smile, she cradled the receiver between shoulder and ear as she uncuffed the sleeve on her robe and smoothed it down her arm. ''Carter residence.''

''Hello, darling. How are you?''

Her smile melted at the sound of the familiar male voice. She dropped her hand from her sleeve to grip the phone against her ear, her stomach knotting. ''How did you know where to find me?''

''Mandy. Though she seemed a bit hesitant to tell me. You aren't still angry with me are you, darling?''

''Angry?'' she repeated, her fingers convulsing on the receiver. ''For what, Marcus? For being an insensitive jerk?''

''Now, Merideth,'' he warned, ''you know how much I detest emotional scenes.''

She sucked in a furious breath. Oh, she knew all right. She could imagine him sitting in his sterile apartment, dressed impeccably as always, his tie knotted perfectly and not a hair out of place. A crystal goblet of wine would be on the beveled glass table at his right and beneath it a marble coaster. Even now he was probably reaching for the glass, centering it perfectly over the circle of marble. Nothing out of order, nothing out of place. She wondered how she'd stood it.

''Yes, you're right of course,'' she said, fighting for calm. ''I'd forgotten.'' But she couldn't resist adding, ''And I'm sure that's why you refused to come to the hospital when you were called.''

''Your sisters were with you. You didn't need me there as well.''

She pressed a fist against her forehead and squeezed her eyes shut, trying to block the memory of that awful day, the terror, the pain, and having to suffer through it all alone for seven hours until Sam and Mandy had arrived. "No, you're right," she said, knowing what he said was true. "I didn't need you." She inhaled deeply, pressing her fingers against her lips. "But you might have at least come for your son's sake. He needed you."

"For Chrissake, Merideth," he said in disgust. "You lost the baby. It wasn't even fully formed."

All the fury, all the resentment that she'd suppressed, boiled up inside Merideth. *"It,"* she screamed in a voice that had Mrs. Baker running into the kitchen to see what was the matter, "was a baby boy. A fully developed baby boy, with ten little fingers and ten little toes. He was your son! Our son!"

"Thankfully, we were spared that," he replied in a voice devoid of emotion. "You know I never wanted children, nor did you, as I recall."

Tears welled, blinding her, but they were for the son she'd lost, not for herself. "You're wrong, Marcus. I wanted him. I loved him."

He cleared his throat, obviously uncomfortable with the direction of the conversation. "I can see that the automobile accident has left you more emotionally scarred than I'd thought. I'd called to discuss a business matter, but perhaps I should postpone the conversation until another time, when you've had a chance to recover fully."

She took a shuddery breath. "Don't bother." With that Merideth slammed the receiver back on its base, then covered her face with her hands. She felt an arm go around her and turned into it, burying her face against Mrs. Baker's shoulder. Deep, heaving, wracking sobs ripped through her.

"There, there," Mrs. Baker soothed. "Have a good cry, if it'll make you feel better." And Merideth did cry, emptying her body, her soul of every emotion she'd suppressed for the last two months. All the grief over the baby she'd lost, the anger, the resentment toward Marcus and his refusal to acknowledge the child they had created together. The loss of the career that she'd worked so hard for. The mess she'd made of her life. When there was nothing left inside, a shudder passed through her, leaving her trembling.

Mrs. Baker took a step back, but kept an arm firmly around Merideth's shoulder. "Come on," she urged gently, guiding Merideth toward the kitchen door. "Let's get you back into bed."

Merideth awakened slowly, feeling as if her face had been dipped in starch. She felt hollow inside, empty, as if someone had drilled a hole and drained the life from her body. She pressed a hand to her cheek, trying to remember.

Then it all came back to her. The call from Marcus. Mrs. Baker holding her while she cried. The dear woman tucking her into bed, with Merideth arguing that she couldn't possibly sleep. But obviously she had.

She had to get up now, she told herself, though the urge to bury her head under the pillow was strong. Mrs. Baker would want to go home and Cassie would need feeding and a bath. Lifting a hand that seemed to be weighted with lead, she pushed back her hair and blinked open her eyes.

John Lee sat opposite her, watching her. He sat so still, his expression so serious that she was sure something terrible had happened.

"Cassie?" she whispered hoarsely, her first thought going to the baby.

''She's fine. Mrs. Baker is feeding her dinner. She thought you needed the rest.''

Closing her eyes, Merideth released a shuddery breath. ''I'm sorry. I didn't mean to fall apart.''

''You were long overdue.''

Merideth opened her eyes to look at him, at that strong handsome face, those deep blue eyes, remembering the hurt, the anger that she'd seen there last. But now she found only compassion. Even as she identified it, he reached for her hand and laced his fingers through hers. Gratefully, almost desperately, she twined her fingers around his.

''Mrs. Baker told me about the phone call,'' he told her. ''Or at least as much as she heard of it.''

Tears budded again, which surprised Merideth. She was sure that she'd cried them all out.

''Do you want to talk about it?'' he asked gently.

''There's really nothing to tell. Marcus is an insensitive ass, but I already knew that.''

''I take it that Marcus was the father of your son?''

Emotion clotted her throat and Merideth could only nod.

Feeling her pain as if it were his own, John Lee squeezed her hand between his. He hated asking and dreaded even more hearing her answer, but he had to know. ''Do you still love him?''

''No. I never did.''

Relief washed through him, though he wondered why her negative response was so important to him. ''Then why the tears?''

''I'm not crying for me,'' she said, trying her best to stem the flow of emotion. ''I'm crying for my baby.'' She picked up the corner of the sheet and dabbed at her cheeks. "Oh, John Lee," she cried. "Can you imagine how awful it must be to never feel loved?"

He cocked his head and frowned.

Knowing she wasn't making any sense, but wanting desperately for him to understand, Merideth tried her best to explain. "Marcus didn't want the baby. He rejected him, both physically and emotionally. He wouldn't even come to the hospital after he'd learned what happened." She pressed the sheet against her lips, tears spilling onto her cheeks. "And I did that to my son. I gave him an insensitive, coldhearted father, a man who couldn't love him."

John Lee moved to sit beside her and pressed their joined hands against his thigh. "Merideth," he soothed, "you aren't responsible for Marcus's emotions, only your own. And you loved your baby, didn't you?"

"Oh, yes," she whispered, clutching the sheet to her heart. "I loved him so much."

"And he felt that love, I'm sure, all through the months you carried him."

Hearing John Lee say that comforted Merideth in a way that nothing had before. She'd been unconscious when her son was born, unable to hold him or welcome him into the world, no matter how brief his stay there. She'd wanted him to know he was loved, and had carried a tremendous guilt that she hadn't been able to give him that assurance.

"He was born almost five months premature and lived less than one hour. I never got to hold him," she murmured sadly, tipping her face up to look at him. "That's why it was so hard for me to hold Cassie at first."

That she'd suffered was obvious. That she'd done so alone, pulled at John Lee's heart. He wanted desperately to say something that would erase all the painful memories, that would bring the light back into her eyes, but could think of nothing.

With no words left to offer, he wrapped an arm around her shoulders. Instead of pulling away as he'd feared she might, rejecting him as she had earlier that day, she leaned into him, resting her head on his shoulder, and laid a hand on his chest. Pressing his head against hers, he covered her hand with his and drew her closer, offering her the only thing he had to give…his comfort.

"We lived together for almost two years," Merideth murmured softly, needing, after holding it inside for so long, to tell John Lee everything. "He was the producer of the show. A handsome man, powerful, but cold." She paused, shivering. "I didn't realize how cold.

"When I discovered I was pregnant, he was furious, and demanded that I have an abortion. I refused and we argued, each hurling accusations at the other. He threatened to cancel my contract, to ruin my career, but I didn't believe he'd do it. I thought the threat was just his way of getting rid of me.

"So I moved out and into a hotel, telling him that I intended to keep the baby, and whether he chose to have a part in the child's life or not was up to him. The weeks that followed were a nightmare." She shuddered, remembering, and John Lee tightened his arm around her.

"I only saw him at the studio, but he made my life a living hell. He found fault with everything I did. My delivery was off, my makeup wrong, my hair too stiff. He had the director call for script changes, changing my lines, cutting me out of more and more scenes as my pregnancy began to show."

She inhaled deeply, her hand clutching John Lee's shirt. "Finally, I'd had enough. I went to his office to confront him, but his secretary refused to let me in. I was determined to have it out with him once and for all, so I stormed past her. When I burst into his office, he was sitting behind his desk, casually sipping a glass of wine. It was as if he was expecting me, as if he'd planned everything to lead up to that point.

"There was an envelope on his desk and he pressed a finger against it and shoved it across the desk. Then he smiled. Not a nice smile, but an evil one." A shiver chased down her spine as if she were seeing it again, feeling its threat. "A letter of severance was inside the envelope and a check. My career was over. Marcus had bought out my contract, ending my career on the show.

"I was furious, but I knew there was nothing I could do. As the producer, he had all the power. So I left. Marcus didn't waste any time stripping me of everything that I'd worked for, that I had earned. When I reached the street, my limousine was gone. Knowing that he was probably watching from his office above, I hailed a taxi. It was raining and the streets were slick and clogged with traffic. We were within a block of my hotel when another car swerved into the lane in front of us."

She pressed a hand to her brow and squeezed. "I don't remember anything after that. Just flashes of sound, the sirens screaming. Voices at the hospital. I remember being wheeled down a corridor and through a set of doors. Then nothing.

"I was told later that they anesthetized me and did an emergency C-section. I must have come to for a moment, because I remember seeing him, my son. Just a flash, really. As if through a thick fog. I remember wanting to hold him, and begging them to please let me, but I couldn't make them understand me. There was a tube in my throat and my hands were strapped to the table. They must have increased the anesthetic then, because I don't remember anything after that. Nothing. Not until the next day, when I came to in the intensive care unit.''

John Lee tightened his arms around her and pressed his lips to the top of her head. ''I'm so sorry, Merideth.''

She inhaled deeply, and realized how much better she felt after talking about it, sharing it all. She squeezed his arm, grateful to him for listening, for caring enough to offer comfort. ''It's okay. Really. I'm better now.'' Even as she said it, she realized it was true. And she had John Lee to thank for that. She pushed away from him, but kept her hands gripped tightly on his arms as she looked up at him.

The smile she offered was a trembly one, but seeing it made John Lee smile in return. ''You're sure?''

She took a deep breath and exhaled it slowly. ''Positive. Thanks to you and Cassie.''

''There's someone here who wants to say hello.''

Merideth and John Lee looked up to find Mrs. Baker standing in the doorway, holding Cassie.

A smile bloomed on Merideth's face and she held out her arms. Mrs. Baker crossed to the bed and passed Cassie to her.

''There's my beautiful little princess,'' Merideth cooed, holding Cassie out in front of her. ''And what have you been doing while I was sleeping?''

Laughing, Cassie kicked her chubby legs and squealed, ''Murrrr.''

Merideth's mouth dropped open. ''Did you hear that?'' she asked, looking up at Mrs. Baker. ''She said Merideth.''

Mrs. Baker just chuckled and turned and left the room.

''John Lee,'' Merideth insisted. ''Did you hear her?''

''Yeah, sugar, I heard her.''

''Don't you think she was trying to say Merideth?''

John Lee pursed his lips thoughtfully, thankful that the storm was over and Merideth was smiling again. "I don't know. Kinda sounded like gas to me."

"Oh, you." Merideth poked him in the ribs with her elbow then sat Cassie down on her lap, drawing the baby's tiny hands between her larger ones. She dipped her face close to hers. "Say it again, sweetheart. Say Merideth."

Cassie looked up at her, her eyes wide, a drip of drool glistening on her lower lip. "Murrr," she said again.

Laughing, Merideth scooped her up and hugged her tight against her. "She did say it!" she cried, and hugged Cassie again. "I told you she could say my name."

John Lee chuckled. "Worst case of gas I've ever heard."

Merideth frowned at him. "You're just jealous because she learned to say my name before she did yours."

He pulled his arm from around Merideth's shoulders and took Cassie from her. "She can say my name. You just haven't heard her." Holding Cassie under her arms, he stood her up on his thighs. "Say John Lee, Cassie," he told her. "Jo-o-ohn Le-e-e-e," he repeated, drawing out the sounds.

She clapped her hands, chortling. "Geeee. Geeee."

John Lee smiled proudly, cocking his head to look at Merideth. "See? What'd I tell you?"

Merideth held out her hands and Cassie reached for her. Smiling smugly, Merideth took her from him and sat her on her lap again. "Yes, but she said my name first."

Eight

Dressed in nothing but a diaper, Cassie played on the floor of the nursery, crawling up and rolling over the life-sized Raggedy Ann, while Merideth lined the drawers of the new dresser with scented paper.

The furniture for the nursery had arrived a couple of days after Mrs. Baker had quit—or after Merideth had fired her, depending on who was telling the story—and Merideth had never had the time to organize the room properly. But with Mrs. Baker back and in charge of the household again, Merideth had the freedom to decorate and organize the nursery to her heart's content.

She'd spent two days on decorating alone, hanging pictures on the wall, drapes at the windows. Another on a shopping spree in Austin with her two sisters while she added to Cassie's growing wardrobe and purchased items for her care. She'd spent hours selecting just the right toys and books to aid in Cassie's physical and mental

development. Mandy had helped, offering advice and
making suggestions, while Sam had paced, muttering that
a kid didn't need all that clutter when a horse could provide her the same dang thing.

Throughout all the days, John Lee had been there, a
solid rock of comfort and support. He'd teased her,
laughed both at her and with her while she'd fretted over
first where to hang pictures in the nursery, then her clum-
siness with a hammer and nail when she'd set about placing them.

He'd kicked and whined like a two-year-old when
she'd asked him to move the furniture in Cassie's room
for the fourth time. And when she'd casually mentioned
that she might like the room painted pink instead of yellow, he'd pitched a walleyed fit, shouting that the paint
wasn't even dry from the last painting and she was already wanting to change it. She'd just laughed and given
him a hug.

To say she was happy would be an understatement,
Merideth knew. She was growing comfortable with her
little makeshift family. She couldn't have loved Cassie
any more if she had been her own. And her feelings for
John Lee...

Merideth's fingers tightened on the footed sleeper she
was folding and she drew it to her breasts. She'd thought
she could control her heart, make herself fall out of love
with John Lee. But she'd been wrong. If anything, her
feelings for him were growing stronger and stronger
every day. She'd always thought him a playboy. A self-
centered, egotistical man with nothing but sex on his
mind. But he was so much more than that. He was kind
and loving and gentle with them all, even Mrs. Baker.
He was funny and fun-loving, yet put in a full day of

work right alongside his men, even when he could have just as easily sat in the house and shouted orders.

Yes, she'd been wrong about John Lee. But then she'd been wrong about a lot of things. So much had changed since she'd first moved in with him to take care of Cassie. And the biggest change was within her.

Pleased with the way her life was going, she held up a dress and a pair of matching panties, the backside of which was covered with rows and rows of pink, frilly lace. A definite improvement over the diapers and T-shirts that Cassie's wardrobe had consisted of prior to her arrival, she told herself with a smile.

Tucking them inside, she closed the drawer and opened another. "And what would you like to wear today?" she asked Cassie as she measured a new length of paper. "The baby-blue bubble with the sun appliqué?" She paused, listening to Cassie's nonsensical jabber, then gave her head a quick nod of agreement. "Excellent choice. Very flattering to your figure and a definite match for your eyes." She slipped the freshly trimmed paper into the drawer, then pushed it closed with her knee.

"There!" she said, dusting off her hands. "Now we can primp." Crossing the room, she scooped Cassie from the floor and swung her high in the air, laughing when Cassie squealed in delight. "You little daredevil," she said and propped her on her hip. "The higher and the faster, the better. You're as bad as your Uncle John Lee."

"She could do worse."

Merideth spun, her heart skipping a beat as she saw John Lee standing in the doorway, his hands braced against the frame. Just looking at him, made her smile. "She's going to be a trapeze artist," she predicted. "She loves to swing high and fast."

"Or maybe a rodeo trick rider," John Lee added, stepping into the room. "I guess I'd better start looking for a pony for her to practice on."

Merideth pressed a hand to her heart. "Oh, please, tell me you're teasing."

Chuckling, he took Cassie from her and lifted her to his shoulder, bracing her back and stomach with his hands. "Every kid needs a pony. You had one."

Merideth frowned, pulling Cassie down from her high perch and settling her safely in the curve of John Lee's arm. "Please don't remind me. I despised that pony. He was mean and vicious and the only reason Daddy bought him for me was because he thought the pony might kill me and save him the trouble."

John Lee's eyebrows shot up. "Merideth McCloud! How can you say such a thing? Your daddy loved you."

She gave Cassie's knee a loving pat, then shrugged philosophically. "In his way, I guess."

He wagged his head. "Yeah, you had it bad all right. Clothes, cars, jewelry. Anything your little heart desired, you mentioned it, and it was yours."

Merideth frowned at the unwanted reminder and folded her arms across her breast. "Materially, yes. But never emotionally." Remembrances of her father's lack of affection for his daughters always filled her with anger, but she refused to allow the memories to upset her today. She pushed arms to her sides and huffed a breath. "I don't want to think about him. It always makes me mad when I do."

John Lee puckered his lips in a low whistle. "Remind me never to get on your bad side."

"Too late. You're already there," she muttered.

He slung an arm around her neck and headed her for the door, determined to tease her out of the dark mood he'd unintentionally brought on. "Name your price. I'll do anything to get back in your good graces."

"Bathe Cassie."

Chuckling, John Lee hugged Merideth to his side, walking with her toward the master bath, certain that he'd been let off easy. "Sugar, your every wish is my command."

Merideth sat on the toilet seat, buffing her nails. "Under her arms, John Lee, and don't spare the soap."

Dodging a spray of water Cassie shot his way, John Lee growled. "You didn't mention anything about me getting a bath, too."

Merideth chuckled. "She likes the water."

"A little too much, if you ask me," he replied dryly. He tried to keep a grip on Cassie's slippery hands while at the same time scrubbing under her arms, and finally succeeded, suffering only a splash or two in the process.

But he forgot about her feet. She lifted both of them and brought them down hard. Water splashed all over his face, momentarily blinding him. He scraped a hand across his face, dragging the corners of his mouth down into a scowl. "You little—"

"Uh-uh-uh," Merideth warned. "Innocent little ears, remember?"

He shot Merideth a murderous look over his shoulder that had her tossing back her head and laughing. Rising, she set aside her nail buffer and gathered a towel over her hands. "That's good enough. Hand her over."

Relieved to be done, John Lee caught Cassie under her arms and pulled her dripping from the water. Merideth quickly whipped the towel around her, cradling her in her arms while she blotted at the child's face with a corner of it. Cassie grabbed the towel and drew it to her mouth, snagging it on that new tooth.

"Isn't she just the most adorable little thing you ever saw?"

John Lee peered over her shoulder to frown at his niece. "Long as she's not near water."

Merideth smiled, stretching the corner of the towel up to swipe a droplet of water from John Lee's cheek. "Don't be such a spoilsport. She was just having a little fun."

"Fun, my—"

Merideth cocked her head in warning.

"—patootie," he said instead, remembering those innocent ears. Reaching for Cassie, he took her from Merideth. "Yeah, she's cute, all right," he said, unable to keep from smiling when she grinned up at him. He tucked her in the curve of his arm and tickled her foot, making her laugh. "And growing by the minute."

Merideth stood on tiptoe to look at Cassie and adjusted the towel over the baby's chest to keep her warm. "Much too fast," she said, suddenly feeling sad. She slipped a hand through the crook in John Lee's arm. "She won't be a baby for long."

Unlacing their arms, John Lee gathered Merideth to his side. "Now don't go getting all teary on me. She's not ready to send off to college, yet."

Merideth pressed her cheek against his shoulder, chuckling. "At least not until she's had her lunch." She tipped up her head to look at him. "How are you with diapers?"

"Who do you think did all the changing before you came along?"

"Good," Merideth said, accepting his answer as a yes. She caught his hand, dragging him along behind her.

"Because you can put a diaper on her while I make us a picnic lunch."

"We're going on a picnic?" he asked, trailing her.

At Merideth's brisk nod, he let out a whoop. "Hot damn—I mean darn! I love picnics!"

Feeling lazy and much too full, John Lee stretched out on the blanket, tucking his hands behind his head. Above him, white, puffy clouds drifted across a turquoise sky. "Did you ever play the cloud game when you were a kid?" he asked curiously.

Merideth tucked the last container into the basket and closed the lid. "Yes," she replied as she crawled across the blanket and to his side. "Lots of times." She stretched out beside him, and tugged one of his hands from beneath his head and stretched his arm beneath her head for a pillow.

He lifted his head high enough to peer at her. "Comfortable?" he asked, arching a brow.

Merideth scooted closer to him and turned her gaze to the sky. "Yes, thank you."

John Lee just shook his head as he looked up at the sky again. You never had to worry about Merideth's comfort. She took care of herself, that was for sure.

"There's a cat," Merideth whispered, pointing at a pattern in the clouds.

John Lee moved his head closer to hers, following the line of her finger. "Where?"

"See his ears? And there's his tail." She moved her finger as if tracing it. "A Persian, judging by how fluffy it is."

"Looks like a bear to me," John Lee commented dryly.

Merideth gave him a poke in the ribs. "It is not! It's

a cat.'' Her eyes widened. ''Quick! Look! See that low cloud moving in? He's licking his paw!''

His attention drawn to her face by the excitement in her voice, John Lee mumbled an uninterested, ''Uh-huh.'' He turned his body a little, angling it toward her, so that he could see her better. Her eyes were narrowed in concentration as she studied the sky, her cheeks flushed by the sun.

She'd have a fit if she got a look at herself in a mirror, he knew. The wind had made a mess of the fancy twist she'd pinned her hair into, and now blond strands brushed her shoulders and brow and curled around her jaw. Her makeup was pretty much shot, too. Her lipstick was gone, her mascara smudged beneath her eyes, and a blob of yellow—probably mustard from their sandwiches, he concluded—stained the corner of her mouth.

But to his way of thinking, she looked good enough to eat…and John Lee was suddenly starving to death.

Almost a week had passed since that god-awful day when her old boyfriend, Marcus, had called. During that time John Lee had kept a safe distance, offering her friendship, but not pushing for anything more as he'd planned to that afternoon out on top of the hill. He hadn't thought it wise, once he understood the emotions she'd had to deal with since that day.

Not that she seemed to have suffered any fallout. As a matter of fact, she seemed happier, more peaceful than he remembered ever seeing her, even before her accident and the loss of her baby. She smiled all the time, laughed like a goon when Cassie did something funny, which seemed pretty regular these days.

At the thought of Cassie, he cocked his head over his shoulder to check on her. She was still snoozing away in the playpen he'd set up for her underneath the tree, her knees drawn up under her, her bottom stuck up in the air, her thumb hanging slack at the corner of her mouth.

Cassie was happier, too, he reflected as he continued to watch her. She didn't fret near as much as she used to and had started making all kinds of weird sounds, which Merideth swore were words. A grin chipped at the corner of his mouth. *Murr*. That seemed to be her name for Merideth, all right. And he was Gee.

Murr and Gee. Stupid-sounding names, but he couldn't help but feel a flush of pleasure every time he heard her say them. Seemed he'd been right in bringing Cassie and Merideth together. They'd been good for each other…and good for him. He'd already been nuts about Cassie, and after Merideth had moved in, well, he'd sort of gotten used to Merideth being around, too.

At the thought, he turned his head back to look at her and found her still studying the sky. She'd laced her fingers across her chest, drawing her index fingers up to form a tall steeple, and tucked her thumbs in the valley between her breasts. As he stared, she heaved a deep sigh and her breasts rose, straining against the yellow T-shirt she wore, her nipples poking up like tightly budded roses.

Hell, he'd gotten more than used to her. He was addicted to her, always plotting ways to steal a kiss from her or just touch her, and fantasizing all the while about making love to her. Just talking to her wasn't so bad, either. She had a razor sharp mind and a quick wit that kept him on his toes all the time. And life was never boring when she was around. She'd be curled up like a kitten against him one minute, purring contentedly, then the next she'd turn on him, clawing and spitting like a she-cat.

That blob of mustard caught his attention again and he couldn't resist the temptation to remove it. He leaned over and swiped at it with his tongue. Startled, Merideth ducked away, drawing up her hands as if to ward off a blow.

John Lee hooted. She'd reacted so quickly, so comically, her eyes so wide with fear, he couldn't help himself.

Immediately, she dropped her hands and tugged her shirt back into place. "What are you cackling about?" she asked irritably, embarrassed by her overreaction.

"You." He tucked his nose against her neck, hiding his smile. "Did you think a snake had crawled up beside you?"

Because that was exactly what she'd thought, Merideth gave his head a rough push. "You just caught me by surprise, that's all."

Still chuckling, he rolled across her, pinning her beneath him. "Are you afraid of snakes, Murr?" he teased.

Hearing him call her by Cassie's name for her made her smile in spite of her irritation with him. "Yes, and I suppose you aren't?"

"They scare the hell out of me." Propping an elbow beside her ear, he dropped his chin on his hand and braced his other hand on her abdomen. "But I thought women liked snakes."

Merideth's eyes widened in dismay. "Whatever would make you think a thing like that?"

He lifted his shoulder in a shrug. "It's in the Bible. As I remember it, Eve and that old snake in the garden of Eden were real chummy."

Merideth snorted a laugh. "Yeah, right."

"They were! In fact, they were such good friends that snake was able to sweet-talk her into eating one of the forbidden apples."

''Yes, and then Eve convinced Adam to eat one, too. And we all know what happened then.''

John Lee grinned. ''We sure do.'' He lowered his head, brushing her nose with his. ''You know,'' he whispered, his breath warming her lips, ''I bet you could talk me into just about anything, just like that old snake talked Eve into eating that apple.''

With his chest all but crushing her, Merideth choked on a laugh. Unable to breathe, she pressed her palm against his chin and pushed him back far enough so that she could look him in the eye. ''If there's a snake in this garden, John Lee Carter, it's you. And if you've got on your mind what I *think* you've got on your mind, you certainly don't need any convincing.''

''Is she asleep?''

Merideth nodded and pulled the nursery door to behind her. ''Out like a light.'' She yawned, stretching her hands above her head as she padded to the bed. ''I'm beat, too.''

John Lee patted the mattress beside him. ''Come on to bed, then.''

Merideth stopped at the side of the bed and folded her arms beneath her breasts, biting back a smile as she looked at him. Naked from the waist up, he sat leaning against the headboard, the sheet pulled across his lap. If he had on anything below the sheet, she'd be surprised…and maybe a little disappointed. ''I thought this was supposed to be *my* bed.''

John Lee grinned. ''It is. But I retained visitation rights.''

Laughing softly, Merideth crawled onto the bed and under the sheets. Scooting her back to the headboard, she settled next to him, then sighed. "What a wonderful day," she murmured dreamily.

"Yeah, it was that, all right. 'Course, there is that one little bit of unfinished business...."

Merideth turned her head to look at him, knowing full well what "business" he was talking about. "Oh? And what would that be?"

He turned and caught her by the waist and dragged her down on the bed until she was flat on her back. "I believe you were lying something like this, while I—" he moved over her, bracing himself above her while he settled his hips against hers "—was somewhere about here."

Laughing, Merideth looped her arms around his neck. "You have such a marvelous memory and eye for detail."

He stretched a hand across the bed and hit a switch on the nightstand. The lights dimmed, shimmering on the walls and ceiling. He hit another one and music swelled from the hidden speakers.

Merideth arched a brow. "Bach? I'm impressed."

"Don't be." He hit another switch and the music faded, then rose again.

Merideth smiled as the sound of George Strait's husky voice accompanied by a single guitar whispered into the room. "That's more like it."

"You like George?" he asked, settling back over her.

"I'm developing an affection for him."

He brushed a knuckle across her cheek, his gaze on hers. "Not too strong an affection, I hope."

She turned her cheek against his hand, enjoying the feel of his skin on hers. "Only as a singer."

"Good. I'd hate to have to break his nose."

She sighed dramatically, clutching his hand in hers. "My hero."

"Aw, shucks, ma'am," he drawled, responding to her playfulness. "I'm no hero. I'm just an old, broken-down cowboy with a blown-out knee."

"I kind of like cowboys," she said and drew his face to hers. She pressed a kiss on his lips, savoring his minty flavor a moment, then drew away, watching her finger's movement on his lower lip as she rubbed the tip of it at the moisture she'd left there. She peeked up at him through long lashes and, at the same moment, slid her hands to the back of his neck. Her nails scraped lightly, teasingly across his wide shoulders, then drifted down his back, firing nerves to life beneath his skin as she passed over them, but stopped at the top of his hips to draw small, light circles there. "Cowboys are so big and strong and have the cutest cowboy butts."

"My, oh my," he whispered huskily as her hands moved to splay over his rump.

A seductive smile played at her lips as she watched his eyes heat, enjoying this bit of power. "You know what, John Lee?"

"What, sugar?" he asked, trying to keep his voice steady.

She tipped up her face to look at the ceiling. "I think I might like to watch."

John Lee's eyes bugged. "Well, I'll be," he murmured.

Before he could make a move to see what he could do about accommodating her request, she'd pushed from beneath him and was standing on the bed, her silk nightgown swirling around her ankles. She jumped and the mattress pitched, jarring John Lee. He rolled to his back to see what she was doing. She jumped again and this time managed to sink her nails into the rosette of knotted fabric, successfully nabbing it. She gave a hard jerk and the knot unraveled, spilling yards of shimmering gold to curtain the bed. She stared up at the mirror she'd uncovered and at John Lee's reflection there. He lay on his side, propped on an elbow, his knees slightly bent, his gaze fixed on the reflection of her upturned face.

He smiled, and she smiled in return. Then she looked away, letting her gaze drift over the length of his reflection. His upper body was tanned a warm, golden brown, but at his waist his skin lightened, a sure sign that he worked without a shirt on at least some of the time. His shoulders, his chest, his arms, his legs...they were all carved by hard muscle, a sculptor's dream.

"Wow," she murmured, turning to look down at him on the bed. "I had no idea a mirror could be so...interesting."

He chuckled and offered her a hand. "Sugar, what you're lookin' at is nothin' but a still life. Wait until the action starts."

Not sure that anything could beat the view she'd just seen, she placed her hand in his and sank to her knees at his side.

"First, let's get rid of this." He caught the hem of her nightgown and, one-handed, stripped it over her head and tossed it aside. His gaze on her breasts, he lifted that same clever hand that had stripped her of her gown and cupped a breast, taking its weight on his palm. She closed her eyes and inhaled deeply, as rivers of sensation flooded through her.

"The idea is to keep your eyes open."

She swallowed hard and forced open her eyes to meet his. "Sorry."

"Nothing to be sorry about. Just didn't want you to miss anything." He gave his chin a jerk upwards, indicating the mirror. "Watch up there," he told her.

Dutifully she tilted her head back until she could see their full forms in the mirror overhead, his hand at her breast. As she watched, he moved his thumb across her nipple, then back again. And again. And again. Until her nipple hardened and reddened beneath his thumb. She could feel the ache, the throbbing heat and would swear later that she could see it, as well.

His hand on her flesh, the contrasts in color, in size, in texture, in strength, coupled with the sensations that flooded her body were almost more than she could bear. Her knees trembled, her hands shook, fire raged over her skin, parching her throat.

She dropped her gaze to his and licked her dry lips. "My turn," she murmured. Planting a hand against his chest, she pushed him to his back and knelt beside him. With her hands at his shoulders, she smoothed her palms in ever-widening arcs down his chest, circling his nipple, teasing him, then flicking a nail against the knotted flesh. He groaned, his body tensing beneath her hands, but Merideth merely smiled and moved her hands on.

Broad at the shoulders, his chest narrowed in a V to his waist. In between there was nothing but hard, muscled flesh. Hooking her hands at his waist, she dragged her hands down his sides, warming the flesh at his hips, his thighs, his calves, her touch nothing but a whisper of sensation by the time her fingertips floated over his toes and disappeared.

She rose, slowly straightening, and tilted back her head, meeting his gaze in the mirror. "You're beautiful," she whispered almost reverently, then lowered her eyes to look down at him on the bed. "So very, very beautiful," she said on a sigh.

In his entire life, John Lee had never been moved so strongly by a mere word. Beautiful. He'd been called a lot of things in his life, some of them not fit for a lady's ears, but no one had ever called him beautiful. If asked, he probably would have laughed to hear the word attributed to a man. But hearing Merideth say it, knowing she was speaking it of him, with all of his scars and bumps and torn ligaments and country ways, touched him in a way that nothing in his life ever had before.

Pushing himself onto one elbow, he reached for her, drawing her to lie by his side. "Merideth..." he whispered huskily before closing his mouth over hers.

She was liquid beneath his heat, a river of sensation that moved with his tide. Calm at moments. Raging at others. Passion slamming at the banks that contained her desire. He filled her, drained her, then filled her again and all with the brush of his lips, the thrust of his tongue.

Her hands strained for him, found him and drew him to her. She felt the weight of his leg on hers, grateful for it, then cursed the confinement. She wanted him in her, with her, moving, rushing toward this dam that restrained her. *Why?* she screamed silently. Why didn't he give her what she wanted, what she needed to end this churning wave of desire that threatened to drown her?

"Merideth."

His voice pulled at her and she fought it, wanting nothing but release.

"Open your eyes."

Heavy. They were so heavy. She couldn't. She didn't want to. She just wanted him. She whimpered, trying to draw him closer, but he remained just out of reach.

"Open your eyes," he said again.

Struggling to do as he asked, she forced open her eyes to meet his gaze. Heat blazed between them, scalding her face, searing her eyes. "John Lee," she begged, her voice a desperate whisper. "Please—"

"Look up," he ordered gently. When she didn't do as he instructed, he pressed a finger beneath her chin, forcing her head back and her face to the ceiling. Her gaze met their reflection on the mirror and she sucked in a ragged breath.

They lay on their sides with their bodies facing each other, their legs twined, his covering hers, their hips mating. Even as she watched, he smoothed a hand down her arm to rest on the swell of her hip, and she shivered, watching and feeling the heat build.

"Keep watching," he whispered, and pressed his mouth against her exposed neck, sipping at her flesh. At the same moment, he rocked his hips forward, joining with her and nipped at the tender flesh at her throat. She gasped as pleasure arrowed through her, and instinctively bowed her back, arching against him, drawing him deeper inside. He moaned against her skin, his breath burning her flesh, then he began to move, rocking his hips against hers, setting the rhythm, the pace.

The muscles of his buttocks corded, then smoothed with each slow thrust and she moved her hand there, feeling the bunch of muscle beneath her palm, kneading the soft flesh with her fingers, watching her hips move with his, helpless to do anything else. Her breath grew shorter and shorter and with it the speed increased, their bodies growing slick with perspiration.

Need grew inside her, and swelled until she was sure she would die. His name echoed in her ears and screamed through her mind and she recognized the voice as her own.

She dug her fingers into his buttocks. "John Lee," she cried, desperate to make him hear. "Ple-e-ease!"

"Now, Merideth," he urged her as he caught her hip in his hand. "Come on, baby," he gasped. "Reach for it.'' With a groan he thrust hard against her, sinking himself deeply inside her and held her against him while he spilled inside her. She cried out, arching, straining toward release and at last found it. She stiffened, then shattered, splitting into a million fragments all bathed in a warm golden glow. Sucking at air, she sagged against him, melting, wilting, her breasts heaving, her heart battering the wall of her chest.

His lips slipped against her neck, then upwards to her chin, moving as he whispered soothing words to her, while his hands kneaded her sated flesh. When his lips found hers, she sighed and combed her fingers through his hair, drawing his face closer still. "Oh, John Lee," she murmured against his mouth. She caught his bottom lip between her teeth and bit down gently, her fingers knotting in his hair as an aftershock of pleasure rocked through her. When it passed, her fingers relaxed their hold on him and she buried her face against his neck with a sigh.

Sated, weakened by their passionate joining, John Lee placed a palm in the hollow of her back and drew her against him. "Stay with me," he murmured against her hair. "Stay here with me and Cassie."

Merideth's heart stopped, then kicked into a rapid beat. Was he asking her to marry him? To accept Cassie as her own? To share with him the responsibilities of parenting? Slowly she drew her head back and looked at him. "What did you say?" she asked.

His face was still flushed with passion, his eyes heavy-lidded as he looked at her. His lips curled in a soft smile. "Stay," he repeated. "Move all your stuff over here. You're good with Cassie and she's crazy about you." His smile deepened and he drew her hips more firmly against his. "And we're pretty good together, too."

Still unsure what he was asking, Merideth tried to keep her face clear of expression, her heart from her eyes. "Is this a proposal?"

His head snapped back, his eyes widening as he stared at her in shock. "As in marriage?"

Her heart plummeted as she realized he wasn't offering her a proposal, but only an open invitation to share his home, his niece, his bed. But her pride wouldn't allow her to show how much that hurt, how much she wanted more.

She rolled away from him, catching up her hair, and sat up, the action giving her time to gather her scattered emotions, to slip the mask back into place. "I had to ask," she replied, proud of the casualness in her tone as she twisted her hair into a knot on top of her head. "Because if it was, I was going to have to figure out a way to let you down easy." She tucked the ends of her hair into the knot, then pulled the sheet to her chin, holding it in place beneath her arms as she settled back against the headboard, the picture of calmness. She forced a smile to her face and looked over at him. "I hate to disappoint you, John Lee, but you're just not the marrying kind."

The bedroom was dark, pitch-black, really, as Merideth lifted her head and listened. Relieved to hear the sound of John Lee's rhythmic breathing, she slipped from the bed and crossed to the nursery. Careful to not make any noise, she twisted the knob, opened the door and slipped inside, then softly closed the door behind her.

She went immediately to the crib and bent over it, looking down at the sleeping Cassie. Tears budded and she laid a hand on the baby's back, absorbing her warmth and measuring the slow steady beat of the baby's heart beneath her palm.

She couldn't stay here, she told herself as the first tear spilled over her lid. She loved them both too much to accept only a temporary spot in their lives.

She knew she would never be satisfied just being a friend to Cassie, or a lover to John Lee. And that was all he was willing to offer her. And she wanted more. So much more. Her mother's heart ached to raise Cassie as her own, to give her all the love and affection that filled her to overflowing each time she looked at the child.

And her woman's heart yearned to give John Lee the same. She wanted to share his life, and hers with him. She wanted to have his children, brothers and sisters for Cassie to play with. She wanted to laugh with him, fight with him, grow old with him. But she also wanted all of him. She knew herself too well to believe that she'd accept anything less. She sniffed, pressing a knuckle against her nose. Oh, God, she cried silently, why does it have to hurt so much?

With her heart breaking, she gently slipped her hands beneath Cassie, lifting her and drawing her into her arms. Her sleep disturbed, Cassie let out a tiny shuddery breath, then shifted, snuggling against Merideth's breasts as she brought her thumb to her mouth.

Crossing silently to the rocker, Merideth sat down, settling Cassie against her, then pressed a bare toe against the thick carpet and set the rocker in motion.

With her gaze on Cassie's sweet angelic face, she held her, rocking slowly back and forth, while tears slid down her cheeks and dripped off her chin. She'd have this memory, she told herself, this night, to take with her and cherish in the lonely days ahead.

* * *

Timing was everything in pulling off a successful performance and Merideth worked furiously, preparing for this final scene. She placed a call to her agent, another to an employment agency, packed her suitcases and called for a limousine...then prayed that all the pieces would fall into place, that her agent would call back with the news that would make this final exit the sweeping success she needed it to be.

She showered and dressed while she awaited his call, taking special care with her makeup to hide the dark circles left from the sleepless night spent crying. She wanted to look her best when she left. She didn't want John Lee's last image of her to be that of a puffy-eyed, hysterical woman, clinging to him and soaking his shirt with her tears. When he thought of her, she wanted his thoughts to be pleasant ones, maybe even tinged with regret.

There'd be no tearful goodbyes. Merideth would see to that. It was all just a matter of control.

The phone rang and Merideth hurried across the den to pick up the extension. She pressed a hand against her heart to still it, before saying, "Carter residence."

"You've got the part. Filming starts next week."

Merideth sagged, bracing a hand against the table to keep herself from going all the way to the floor. "Oh, Stephen, thank you! You're the best."

"Don't thank me. *You're* the one with the talent. When you left New York and said you were never coming back, I told you we could go anywhere we wanted and name our price."

Merideth sighed, remembering the conversation. But at the time she hadn't wanted to go anywhere but home.

"I'm flying out today," she told him. "I'll call you when I arrive."

"Reservations are already made for you at the hotel and there'll be a limo at the airport, waiting for you. The studio sent the scripts directly to the hotel, so they'll be there when you arrive. We'll give you a couple of weeks to settle in, then we'll start looking for a place of your own."

Merideth pressed her hand to her forehead, dizzy at the speed with which things were coming together. "Heavens! I'm not even there and you have me buying real estate."

He chuckled. "You just get on the plane to California. I'll take care of the rest."

She smiled, her lips trembling a little, grateful for his help. "Thanks, Stephen."

The front door opened and Merideth looked up to see John Lee in the doorway, swiping the soles of his boots on the mat there. Her heart rose to her throat at the sight of him, knowing she would soon be telling him goodbye. She swallowed hard, forcing back the emotion, the regret.

John Lee stepped inside, closing the door behind him, then frowned when he nearly tripped over the luggage stacked beside the door. He lifted his head, his gaze meeting hers, and she forced a bright smile.

"Listen, Stephen," she said into the receiver. "I've got to run. I'll call you when I arrive."

John Lee circled the luggage and tossed his hat onto the entry-hall table as she hung up the phone. "You going somewhere?"

Merideth clasped her hands beneath her chin and squealed. "Oh, John Lee, you aren't going to believe what has happened! My agent called and I've been offered a part in a made-for-television movie!"

John Lee took the news like a blow to his chest. He glanced back at the luggage and his palms began to sweat. Slowly, he turned his gaze back to hers. "So you're leaving?"

"Yes!" She all but danced across the room to grab his hand. "Filming starts next week and I've got a zillion things to do to prepare."

Though her excitement was obvious, for the life of him, John Lee couldn't work up so much as a smile. "Isn't this sort of sudden?"

"Yes!" she laughed, giving his hand an excited squeeze. "My head is still spinning! I've never done film before, just television and stage. This could be the beginning of a whole new career." She pressed a hand to her heart and sighed dramatically, her eyes going dreamy. "I can just see it now. My name in lights."

Slowly, John Lee pulled his hand from hers. "But what about us—I mean, what about Cassie? Who's gonna look after her if you hightail it to California?"

Though his question nearly brought her to her knees, Merideth kept her smile in place, her emotions carefully masked. She looped her arm through his and tugged him into the den with her, knowing she had to do this quickly, or she'd never pull off the charade. "Don't worry," she assured him. "I'm not leaving you in the lurch. I've called an employment agency and they're sending out three women today for you to interview as a possible nanny for Cassie.

"I've screened all the applicants myself over the phone and checked their references. All are qualified, have experience and come with glowing references from their former employers."

She dropped his arm to pick up her purse, frowning as she dug through its contents for her lipstick. "I'll leave the final decision up to you," she told him, smiling as she found the tube and withdrew it. She gave it a twist, and a creamy stick popped up, the color of fresh, ripe raspberries. Plucking a small mirror from her purse, she closed John Lee's fingers around it and drew his hand up in front of her face, eyeing her reflection. "But I do think that you should involve Cassie in the decision-making process.

"Have her in the room during the interviews and allow her to interact with each of the women. Study her expressions, her body movements and see which of the women she responds to the best." She parted her lips, and slightly puckered them, then traced their shape with the lipstick. Tucking her chin back, she studied her reflection critically, then, satisfied, dropped the tube of lipstick back into her purse.

John Lee's fingers tightened on the mirror, desperation slowly setting in. "Now listen, sugar, if it's the money, I'll match whatever those damn producers are offering you, and you can stay right here on the ranch with us."

Merideth's mouth dropped open at the offer. "Stay on the ranch?" she repeated in disbelief, then tossed back her head and laughed. "Darling, I'm an actress, not a nanny!"

She watched his frown deepen, his face redden, and silently whispered a prayer of thanksgiving when a horn sounded out front before he had time to form a response.

"Oh, heavens! That must be my driver!" She snatched the mirror from John Lee's hand and dropped it back into her purse. "Mrs. Baker!" she shouted. "My car is here. Would you please bring Cassie so I can tell her goodbye?"

She ran to the door and threw it wide, beaming a smile at the chauffeur who was climbing the steps. "My luggage is all right here," she told him, ushering him inside.

"And please be a dear and place the garment bag on top, so it doesn't get crushed."

Slipping her purse strap over her shoulder, she snagged her makeup case from the top of the hall table and followed the heavily burdened driver out onto the porch.

John Lee followed, with Mrs. Baker hot on his heels, Cassie propped on her hip.

Taking a deep breath, Merideth turned to them, knowing she had to make this exit fast before her mask cracked. "Well," she said, smiling radiantly, and spreading her arms wide. "This is it!" She took Cassie from Mrs. Baker and held her up high in the air for a moment before drawing her tight against her breasts for a hug. Fighting the surge of emotion that threatened, she lectured gently, "Now, you be a good girl for Mrs. Baker." She drew the baby back to look at her. "And remember what I told you," she said, pressing the tip of her finger against the tip of Cassie's nose. "Blue is your best color and avoid yellows of any kind."

She gave her another quick squeeze and passed her back to Mrs. Baker, then wrapped her arms around both Mrs. Baker and Cassie, hugging them close. As she withdrew, she swiped the pad of her thumb across a smudge of lipstick she'd left on Mrs. Baker's cheek.

"On occasion," she whispered, as if sharing some deep, dark secret, "the men like to have their butter cut into little florets. Indulge them. But whatever you do, don't slice the crusts from their bread. It makes them grouchy." She bit back a smile then gave the woman another peck on the cheek.

With her lips pressed tightly together to hide their trembling, Mrs. Baker gave Merideth a brisk nod, then caught up the hem of her apron and dabbed at a tear at the corner of her eye. Merideth turned away quickly, unsure how much longer she could keep up the charade.

Only John Lee remained between her and the limousine. She forced an even higher wattage of brightness into her smile and braced her hands at her hips. "Well, this is it, cowboy," she said, all sass. "Pucker up." Laughing, she leaned and bussed a quick kiss on his lips, then whirled and ran down the steps to the waiting limousine. She'd almost reached its open door when an arm grabbed her from behind and swung her around.

She barely had time to draw in a startled breath before a muscled set of arms closed around her, hauling her up hard against a wall of muscled chest. The sun disappeared behind a sandy blond head just before John Lee's mouth hit hers hard, his lips bruising, his teeth scraping. Bent backwards, she fisted her hands in his shirt and clung.

The kiss only lasted seconds. A lifetime. Then John Lee withdrew and looked down at her, his eyes boring straight into her soul. "Just thought you might need something to remember me by," he said, his voice husky. Then he released her and stepped back, bracing a hand on the open door.

Her knees shaking, Merideth slipped inside the limousine and settled back against the leather seat. The door closed and she reached over, pressing a finger against the window release, and the tinted glass glided down. Scooting forward on the seat, she looked up at John Lee. "See you, cowboy." Pressing two fingers against her lips, she blew him a kiss, then waved as the limousine pulled away.

Leaning back, she pressed a fingertip against the release, raising the window. She didn't look back, she didn't dare, but kept her eyes focused on the back of the chauffeur's head. "At the highway," she instructed, her voice trembling, "take a right, then watch for a sign for the Double-Cross Heart Ranch. I need to stop there and tell my sisters goodbye."

"Yes, ma'am."

Merideth pressed the button that raised the tinted window between her and her driver, then settled back. The tears came quickly, flooding her eyes, streaming down her cheeks, and she did nothing to stop their flow. She deserved to cry. She'd just put on the best performance of her entire career. And if her heart was breaking, no one would ever know.

Nine

He was dying, he was sure of it. He had this pain in his chest that ached worse than any he'd ever had in his knee. He couldn't eat. Couldn't sleep. Couldn't think.

Well, the last was a lie. He could think, all right. And it was what he was thinking that was causing all the rest of his symptoms. Merideth. The damn woman haunted his every step.

She was everywhere. In his bedroom, in his bathroom, in his car. He couldn't even eat his breakfast without imagining her as she'd stood that morning when he'd gone out early to drive to Austin for that tractor part. A vision of seduction standing there in his kitchen in that piece of nothing of a nightgown, her lips all pouty and sweet, her nipples nudging that thin strip of lace.

He got hard just thinking about it.

And her scent! No amount of scrubbing could erase it. He knew, because he'd tried. He'd used two bottles of a pine-scented cleaner on his bathroom, thinking if he couldn't scrub it off, at least he could smother it. But he still smelled her at every turn.

The mirror above his bed was creating a whole different set of problems. He couldn't sleep for looking in it, seeing Merideth there all naked and hot, her body tangled with his, watching her hands trail over his body, watching her hips move in rhythm with his. As much as he liked his mirror, he was afraid he was going to have to tear the dang thing down.

Cassie sure wasn't helping much, either. Blubbering "Mur-r-r" all the time, and looking so pitiful he thought his heart would break. He'd catch her sometimes, looking around kind of hopeful as if she expected Merideth to come sashaying into the room at any moment.

The nursery was another can of worms he had to deal with. He couldn't take a step inside without looking at that rocker and seeing Merideth sitting there with Cassie in her lap, humming some little song while she rocked Cassie to sleep. Other times, he'd remember the day they'd gone nose-to-nose over what she'd referred to as his "toys," saying Cassie needed her own room, her own things so she'd feel more secure in her new home.

Well, if she was so damn worried about Cassie feeling secure, then why the hell did she run off and leave her? he asked himself furiously. Cassie needed her. She loved her.

He loved her.

He froze, then gulped. Loved her? Blowing out a breath, he sank down on the hay bale, his knees weak. He sat there a moment, letting it sink in, even trying to talk himself out of it. But he couldn't. A man couldn't argue with facts. And the fact was, he loved her.

The realization had no sooner formed than he was

jumping to his feet. He'd go and get her, he told himself. Haul her back to Texas where she belonged. They'd get married. They'd—

He sagged back down again, curling his hands around the hay bale's edge to keep himself from pitching over onto the floor in a dead faint. Married? Him? John Lee Carter?

He dragged a hand across the sweat that popped up on his forehead. He couldn't get married. He didn't want to get married. He liked his freedom. No. He *loved* his freedom. Women were his hobby. His pastime. His joy. He loved 'em, all of 'em, and they loved him. He'd go stark raving crazy if he was chained to the same woman for the rest of his life.

He gave his head a shake, freeing himself of thoughts of marriage and Merideth. "Whew! That was a close one, Carter," he muttered with a nervous laugh, and gave his heart a soothing pat. He'd come dang close to making the biggest mistake of his life. Taking off for California and bringing Merideth back. Marrying her. What was he thinking?

He just needed a night out, he told himself. A little loving with a willing woman and he'd be back to normal in no time. He stood up again, though his knees—both the good and the bad one—still trembled a little. He'd call one of his friends. Maybe Muffy. He hadn't seen her in...

He stopped, frowning, trying to remember the last time he'd seen Muffy. He scratched his head, hoping to shake loose a memory of her or another woman he'd seen recently. Anybody! But durned if he could think of a one. It had been months since he'd been out with a woman. And the oddest thing of all was that he hadn't even noticed or felt deprived.

It was because Merideth had been there, he realized. Not once during the entire time she'd been living with him had he even thought about another woman, much less gone out with one.

He tried to work up the enthusiasm to head on up to the house and give Muffy a call…but he couldn't.

He dropped his chin to his chest. It's no use, he told himself. He didn't want to see Muffy. Or Debbie. Or Trish. Or Suzanne. Or any other woman, for that matter. He'd lost his taste for any woman other than Merideth.

He rubbed a hand against the ache in his chest. He wanted Merideth. She was the only woman for him. And some way or another, he was going to have her.

He sat down on the bale again, his rear end sinking into the nest he'd shaped with all his yo-yoing up and down, wondering if he'd be able to talk her into coming home with him and marrying him. It'd be a hard sell. She hated ranch life. He knew that for a fact. She'd run from her own home years before just to escape it.

And would it be fair to ask her to give up her career? he asked himself. She loved acting, and had made a real success of it. He remembered the expression on her face when she'd told him about this new offer for a made-for-television movie. All bright-eyed and smiling.

He rose slowly, firming his lips, remembering her standing on his front porch, her hands braced on her hips, full of sass and saying, "Well, this is it, cowboy. Pucker up." At the time, he'd been so choked with the thought of her going, so shocked that she'd even consider leaving them, that he hadn't said anything, hadn't tried to stop her or persuade her to stay.

But he wasn't choked up now. He was mad. Dang mad. Putting him and Cassie through such misery. Making them miss her. And all the while she was off having herself a high old time in Hollywood.

He grabbed up his hat and rammed it on his head. Not for long she's not, he told himself, because he was going to California and he was bringing her home where she belonged, whether she wanted him to or not.

And if she put up a fuss… Well, he hoped she did. He was ready to go another round or two with Miss Merideth McCloud.

"A cowboy, huh?"

Merideth stared miserably at her reflection in the mirror and nodded while the makeup artist dabbed, buffed and dabbed again, trying to conceal the red puffiness around her eyes.

"I've always wondered what it would be like to date a cowboy. Is he worth all these tears?"

Merideth's lower lip began to tremble.

"Oh, no you don't," the woman warned, seeing the swell of tears. "I've already patched your makeup twice this morning and I'm not doing it again."

Merideth hiccuped a sob. "But—"

Before she could say another word, the woman gave the chair a hard twist, then hopped out of the way. Merideth's mouth gaped, her head snapped back and she dug her nails into the chair's padded arms to keep from being catapulted across the room.

"Trixie Starr!" she screamed as the chair spun crazily. "You stop this thing right this minute!"

"Are you going to cry any more?"

Merideth shot the woman a murderous look as she spun past her, but Trixie just laughed and gave the chair another hard push.

"No! Please!" Merideth begged, her stomach beginning to churn. "I won't cry."

"Promise?"

"Promise," she whimpered weakly.

Trixie grabbed the back of the chair as it swung past and dragged it to a stop.

Her head still whirling, Merideth struggled to pull herself back to a sitting position. When she had, her chest swelled and all hell broke loose. "Trixie Starr, you are the meanest, the vilest, the most despicable person I've ever met in my life! I ought to have you fired!"

Trixie rolled her eyes and flapped a hand. "Yeah, yeah. Tell it to somebody who cares."

Furious, Merideth snatched a tissue from the box on the vanity and pressed it beneath her nose. As she did, she met Trixie's gaze in the mirror. The redhead stood behind her, her arms folded across her chest, her mouth puckered smugly. A smile trembled on Merideth's lips, then, unable to help herself, she burst out laughing.

"You did that on purpose, didn't you?"

Trixie lifted a shoulder. "You aren't crying any more, are you?"

"Who could cry when their breakfast is threatening a return performance as their lunch?"

Trixie chuckled and picked up a makeup brush. She dipped it into a pot of concealer and started over again, dabbing it beneath Merideth's eye. After only two strokes, Merideth touched her hand, stopping her.

"Thank you."

Trixie grinned. "For giving you the ride of your life?"

Merideth smiled. "No. For being my friend."

Trixie scrunched her nose, obviously embarrassed. "It's a tough job, but somebody's got to do it."

The door opened behind them, and a runner called, "Two minutes, Miss McCloud."

"I'll be right there."

Trixie quickly repaired the damage then whipped the smock from around Merideth's shoulder. "Break a leg."

Merideth stood and checked her reflection, giving her hair one last fluff, then turned and gave Trixie a quick hug. "I owe you one," she whispered, then released her and hurried back to the set.

John Lee shifted Cassie to his opposite hip and carefully made his way through the web of cables snaking across the floor. Stopping behind an unmanned camera, he used it for concealment as he stole a glance at the set. He saw her almost instantly...and silently cursed her for looking so damn beautiful.

Obviously, she wasn't suffering sleepless nights, haunted days, like he was. He narrowed an eye at the skimpy cocktail dress she was wearing.

"Mur-r-r," Cassie cried, clapping her hands.

John Lee ducked behind the camera and clamped a hand over her mouth, burying his mouth at her ear. "Shhh. Remember?" he whispered to her. "This is supposed to be a surprise."

He glanced around to see if anyone had noticed them, but fortunately there was a lot of noise and everyone seemed pretty consumed with whatever task they were about. Relieved, he dropped his hand and dug in his pocket for the pacifier.

"Here, Princess. Suck on this for a while," he whispered and popped it into her mouth.

"Places, everyone. Places."

There was a flurry of movement as people scurried in all directions, then silence. John Lee peeped around the side of the camera. Only Merideth and some slick-haired man wearing a tux remained on the stage. Another guy dressed in jeans darted in front of them, holding a clapboard, and shouted "Scene five, take three," then disappeared.

Instantly, the action started. The man on the stage grabbed Merideth and put a lip lock on her that had John Lee's eyes bugging, then narrowing to dangerous slits. "So much for foreplay," he muttered under his breath, then nearly choked when the man put his hands on Merideth's shoulders, caught the thin straps that held up her dress and began to peel them down her arms.

As far as John Lee was concerned, this scene had played long enough. With a low growl, he stepped around the camera and strode for the set. He knocked over an umbrella light stand, shoved a cameraman aside, and elbowed his way past some owl-eyed woman holding a script. Another two steps and he was on the set.

He shifted Cassie to his opposite hip, grabbed the man's arm, swung him around, reared back and planted his fist right square in the man's face. The guy toppled like a stack of bricks.

Her eyes wide in horror, Merideth watched him fall, then slowly turned. Her eyes widened even more when she saw John Lee. "What are you doing here?" she asked in a shocked whisper.

Scowling, he shook his stinging fist. "I came to take you home."

"Cut! Cut!"

"Somebody call security!"

"Is Shaun okay?"

"Kill the lights!"

A moan came from the guy on the floor.

Someone grabbed John Lee from behind and Merideth

snatched Cassie from him just as he stumbled backwards, his arms pinned behind his back. "No," she cried, grabbing at the security man's arms. "It's okay. I know him."

Another guy, the director, John Lee figured, came streaking onto the stage. "What is the meaning of this?" he shouted angrily.

Merideth melted into a puddle of apologetic mush. "Oh, Ted, I'm sorry. I'm afraid there's been a terrible misunderstanding. If you'll give me a few minutes, I'm sure I can get it all straightened out."

Ted shot John Lee a scowl, which John Lee gladly returned, then the director turned and yelled. "Lunch break! Everybody back on the set in one hour."

The hands that held John Lee's arms behind him disappeared. Turning to frown at the security guard's back as he walked away, John Lee gave his cuffs a snap, tugging his shirtsleeves back into place.

It took two people to help the moaning Shaun up from the floor, and John Lee thought he heard the guy mumble something about a lawsuit, but he didn't care. The satisfaction he'd gotten from burying his fist in the guy's face was well worth whatever it cost him in fines.

Within seconds, the place was empty, leaving only Merideth, John Lee and Cassie on the set. Merideth cupped a protective hand at Cassie's back and whirled on John Lee, her eyes blazing. "What are you trying to do? Ruin my career?"

John Lee stuck his hands in his pockets, and scuffed the toe of his boot against a line of cable. "No, not exactly."

"Then what did you hope to gain? Storming in here like some kind of maniac, slugging my leading man." She pressed a hand to her brow, seeing it all again—

Shaun crumpling, her director's furious face. She dropped her fingers to press them on her trembling lips. "I'm ruined," she moaned miserably.

John Lee scowled. This wasn't the welcome he'd hoped for. "I didn't plan on hitting him."

She snapped her head up to glare at him. "Well, you did," she reminded him furiously.

He propped his hands on his hips and glared right back. "Well, what'd you expect me to do? The guy had his tongue halfway down your throat!"

Merideth's mouth dropped open. "He most certainly did not!"

"Damn close," he replied resentfully.

She snapped her lips together and glared at him. "You're just jealous," she accused him.

"Jealous! Of that pansy-faced actor?"

The accusation had been a reflex for Merideth, a means of getting in her own dig, but the speed and bluster of John Lee's response told her that she was right. He was jealous. And the thought that he would be thrilled her! She tossed back her head and laughed. "You *are* jealous!"

John Lee scowled. "Well...maybe a little. But the guy was enjoying himself way too much. Besides," he added, nodding toward Cassie, "I don't think Cassie ought to be seeing that kind of stuff. Might give her nightmares or something."

If Merideth hadn't already been in love with him, she would have fallen in love with him at that moment. She crossed to him and laid a hand on his cheek. "Oh, John Lee," she murmured, "you didn't have to hit him. It was all just an act."

"Could've fooled me," he mumbled.

Sighing, she withdrew her hand and wrapped her arms

around Cassie, her anger with him gone. "Why are you here, John Lee?" she asked softly.

He stuffed his hands in his pockets again and used his shoulder to gesture toward Cassie. "She misses you."

Merideth tucked her chin back to smile at Cassie. "Do you miss me, darling?" Cassie pulled out her pacifier and tried to stick it in Merideth's mouth. Laughing, Merideth caught it in her hand and hugged Cassie to her. "Well, I've missed you, too."

"And she wants you to come back home with us where you belong."

Merideth's heart stopped for a moment, then kicked furiously against her ribs. Slowly she looked up at him. "Home?" she repeated.

With his hands still stuck in his pockets like they were glued there, John Lee frowned. "Yeah, home."

"B-but why?"

"I already told you," he muttered impatiently. "Cassie misses you. Cries all the time."

That he was using Cassie as a shield to hide his own emotions behind was obvious, and it infuriated Merideth. The stubborn man! Well, she wouldn't let him get away with it. If he wanted her in Texas with him, then by golly he would have to say so. "So you're here to take me home for a visit. Is that it?"

He heaved a frustrated breath. "Not for a visit. We came to *take* you home. You know, permanent-like."

"Why?"

He ripped his hands from his pockets and gestured wildly. "For God's sake, Merideth! Are you listening to anything I'm saying? Cassie misses you. She needs you. She wants you back home where you belong."

"And what do *you* want, John Lee?" she asked pointedly.

"The same damn thing."

Merideth was sure she was going to scream. But she wouldn't. He'd say it all, if she had to pluck every single word out of him with tweezers. "And I'm supposed to walk off this set, break a signed contract and ruin my career, just because Cassie misses me?"

"Ah, hell, Merideth," he whined. He reached for Cassie and took her from Merideth's arms. "She loves you. We both do. And we want you back home with us, where you belong."

It wasn't an out-and-out declaration of love, although it was awfully close for a man like John Lee...but not anywhere close enough for Merideth. She'd already suffered through one mistaken proposal from him and she wouldn't suffer through another one.

"What is it you want from me, John Lee? A full-time nanny for Cassie? A live-in lover for you?"

He spun away in frustration, then whirled back, hooking Cassie at his hip. "Has all this smog affected your hearing or something? For God's sake, Merideth, I'm asking you to be my wife and Cassie's mother!"

Stunned that he'd finally said the words she'd so desperately needed to hear, Merideth stared, afraid to trust her ears. "Your wife?" she repeated.

"Yes, my wife!" John Lee hauled in a calming breath, then blew it out real slow. This wasn't how he'd planned to propose to her—not that he'd had a plan in mind when he'd taken off for California to bring her home. But he sure as hell hadn't expected to scream his proposal at her, and judging by the shocked look on her face, he figured he'd messed things up royally.

"Listen, sugar," he said, hoping to make her see things his way. "I know this sounds like I'm asking you to give up a lot, and I guess I am, but I'm willing to compromise where I can. If you'll just say you'll marry me, we—

"Yes!" Merideth threw herself at him, wrapping her arms around both him and Cassie, laughing. "Yes, yes, yes, yes!"

Stumbling back a step, John Lee managed to get an arm around her waist, steadying them all before they toppled over. Grinning, he craned his neck back to look at her. "Well, I'll be damned," he murmured.

Merideth pressed a kiss first on Cassie's cheek, then a more passionate one on John Lee's mouth. She drew back, leaving a hand curled behind his neck and another pressed over his heart. "What took you so long to come after me?" she asked, tears stinging her eyes. "I've been absolutely miserable without you two."

John Lee's forehead plowed in confusion. "But, sugar, I thought this is what you wanted? You seemed so excited at the prospect of making a movie."

Merideth dropped her gaze to his chest. She traced the outline of his shirt pocket with a manicured nail. "That was just an act," she admitted reluctantly. "I couldn't bear the thought of being only a temporary part of your and Cassie's lives. Leaving seemed less painful than staying."

John Lee tucked her head against his chest and hugged her to him. "Aw, sugar."

"But you know what?" she murmured, comforted by the steady beat of his heart. "When I wasn't missing you and Cassie, I really have enjoyed the challenge of making a movie. It's so different from the acting that I've done before. And I'd really like to finish this project."

"And you will," John Lee promised her.

"But how?" she asked, lifting her head to look at him. "I can't be two places at once."

He frowned and tightened his arm around her. "Well, I don't know exactly. But it doesn't seem fair that you have to give up everything, when Cassie and I get to go along just like we were. Surely there's a compromise in here somewhere. We'll just have to find it."

An idea began to form in Merideth's mind. She took a step back, turning away from him, then spun around to face him again. "Did you hire one of the nannies I had the employment agency send out?"

John Lee swelled his chest. "Sure did. And a good one, too. Just like you told me to."

"Does she like to travel?"

"Well, I don't know," he said uncertainly. "Was that one of the questions I was supposed to ask her?"

Merideth shook her head. "No, but if she doesn't, we may have to hire a new one."

"Whatever you say, sugar."

Merideth laughed at his easy acquiescence and threw her arms around him, including Cassie in the embrace. "Don't you see, John Lee? We can use the ranch as our home base, and when I have to be away on location, Cassie and her nanny can travel with me. We can fly home for the weekends, or you can join us when you can. And it isn't as if we'll be gone all the time. I can limit the number of projects I do a year."

He stepped back, keeping a hand on her to hold her at arm's length. "On one condition," he cautioned her.

"What?"

"You have to have a stand-in for all those love scenes."

Merideth threw her arms around his neck, laughing. "Oh, I love you, John Lee Carter."

He hitched Cassie up higher on his hip and smiled smugly. "Yeah, I know."

Merideth gave his chest a shove and pouted. "You're supposed to say you love me, too."

Working an arm around her waist, he turned her and headed her toward the studio door. "Sugar, you know I love you. Hell, I'm crazy about you. But I'm a man of action. I'd rather *show* you how much I love you. Now, have you got one of those little casting couches in your dressing room? You know, the kind where the leading man is supposed to seduce his leading lady?"

Laughing, Merideth slipped her arm around his waist and hugged him to her. "Not only that, I have a wonderful friend named Trixie who I know would love to baby-sit for a couple of hours."

He stopped, pulling her to a stop too. He dipped his head over hers and branded her with a kiss that burned all the way to her toes.

Dragging her lips from his, she looked up at him. "What was that for?" she asked breathlessly.

He grinned and tugged her on toward the dressing room. "Sugar, where I come from, we call it foreplay."

*   *   *   *   *

SILHOUETTE
DESIRE®

COMING NEXT MONTH

SLOW-TALKING TEXAN Mary Lynn Baxter

Man of the Month

Tycoon Porter Wyman could handle complex business deals, but as a single dad he was at a loss! Still, with Ellen Saxton's help he was sure he could manage… How much trouble could one baby be?

DEDICATED TO DEIRDRE Anne Marie Winston

Ronan Sullivan needed a place to stay, and Deirdre Patten had a room to rent. But he hadn't told her he was wealthy enough to buy a mansion! Ronan wanted to be sure her passion was for *him*—not his money…

THE CONSUMMATE COWBOY Sara Orwig

Zach Durham had the ability to inspire desire in women who should know better—including Emily Stockton. This sexy man had her heart racing and her mind reeling… But as her sister's ex, surely he was off-limits?

THE NON-COMMISSIONED BABY Maureen Child

Bachelor Battalion

Captain Jeff Ryan fought a lot of battles as a marine. But when a baby was left on his doorstep, he faced his toughest assignment ever! Until he called in reinforcements in the form of nanny Laura Martin…

COWBOYS DO IT BEST Eileen Wilks

Chase McGuire knew he shouldn't seduce his new boss. But he couldn't help wanting her! What's more, he knew Summer Callaway needed him. Her life was in danger—and so was her child's!

THE TEXAS RANGER AND THE TEMPTING TWIN
Pamela Ingrahm

Quinn O'Byrne's mission was to get close to Kerstin Lundquist to find her sister—a suspect. But soon he'd fallen hard for the tempting twin, and he wished he could tell her who he really was…

9907

COMING NEXT MONTH FROM

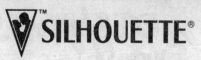 **SILHOUETTE®**

Sensation

A thrilling mix of passion, adventure and drama

THE BADDEST BRIDE IN TEXAS Maggie Shayne
MURPHY'S LAW Marilyn Pappano
EVERYDAY, AVERAGE JONES Suzanne Brockmann
ONE MORE KNIGHT Kathleen Creighton

Intrigue

Danger, deception and desire

SOMEBODY'S BABY Amanda Stevens
SPENCER'S SECRET Laura Gordon
THE MISSING HOUR Dawn Stewardson
MYSTERY DAD Leona Karr

Special Edition

Compelling romances packed with emotion

OPERATION: BABY Barbara Bretton
THE WINNING HAND Nora Roberts
A FAMILY KIND OF GIRL Lisa Jackson
FROM HOUSE CALLS TO HUSBAND Christine Flynn
PRENUPTIAL AGREEMENT Doris Rangel
AKA: MARRIAGE Jule McBride

4 FREE

books and a surprise gift!

We would like to take this opportunity to thank you for reading this Silhouette® book by offering you the chance to take FOUR more specially selected titles from the Desire™ series absolutely FREE! We're also making this offer to introduce you to the benefits of the Reader Service™—

- ★ FREE home delivery
- ★ FREE gifts and competitions
- ★ FREE monthly Newsletter
- ★ Exclusive Reader Service discounts
- ★ Books available before they're in the shops

Accepting these FREE books and gift places you under no obligation to buy, you may cancel at any time, even after receiving your free shipment. Simply complete your details below and return the entire page to the address below. **You don't even need a stamp!**

YES! Please send me 4 free Desire books and a surprise gift. I understand that unless you hear from me, I will receive 6 superb new titles every month for just £2.70 each, postage and packing free. I am under no obligation to purchase any books and may cancel my subscription at any time. The free books and gift will be mine to keep in any case.

D9EA

Ms/Mrs/Miss/Mr ....Initials....................................
BLOCK CAPITALS PLEASE

Surname ....

Address ....

....

....Postcode................................

Send this whole page to:
THE READER SERVICE, FREEPOST CN81, CROYDON, CR9 3WZ
(Eire readers please send coupon to: P.O. BOX 4546, DUBLIN 24.)

MAN OF THE MONTH

Look out for Desire's™ hottest hunks! Every month we feature our most sensual and sizzling man in a specially marked book.